Roger T Lena

GENERATION WILD, YES, WE ARE

Limited Special Edition. No. 1 of 25 Paperbacks

The author was born in Kinshasa, capital of Democratic Republic of Congo. He came to France in 1982 to continue his study in university. But in 1998, he decided to move to UK with the aim to learn English.

Generation Wild, Yes, We Are is his first book.

Glory be to GOD for helping me renew my intelligence. May God bless the 'Grace Ministry' where I worship every Sunday in Portsmouth. Thank you to my wife, Clarisse Lecken, and my lovely two children, Beverley and Cleverley, for their moral and spiritual support. Huge thanks to all colleagues and carers in Portsmouth for their hard job, to Sir David Attenborough and to Diane Fossey.

Roger T Lena

Generation Wild, Yes, We Are

Austin Macauley Publishers™
London • Cambridge • New York • Sharjah

A CIP catalogue record for this title is available from the British Library.

ISBN 9781528912310 (Paperback)
ISBN 9781528960083 (ePub e-book)

www.austinmacauley.com

First Published (2020)
Austin Macauley Publishers Ltd
25 Canada Square
Canary Wharf
London
E14 5LQ

Table of Contents

Foreword

This book has been written, firstly, to be a book of entertainment, and secondly, to raise awareness about the cruelty humans inflict on animals. For example, those who enjoy hunting and eating exotic animals. Through this book, I wish to convey the idea of considering animals as companions in life and respecting them as fellow beings. In nature, where both humans and animals live alongside one another, both have a right to survive. Due to cultural or social influences, some people view animals as solely a source of food, without any inclination to respect them. However, other people who understand the reality of life must take it upon themselves to explain to others why killing animals for profit; for example, the Ivory trade, skins or aphrodisiacs, is morally wrong.

In this book, I've shown what animals would say if they could talk and express their feelings in a comical way so that the reader can empathise with them. 'Virunga Park' is a cosmopolitan place where human beings and animals rub against each other and create a unique atmosphere.

Chapter 1
Betty, the Bird

All around the world, people immigrate. They travel to seek a better life away from their homeland. This striving to find a better life is not just exclusive to humans; animals and Birds are also constantly moving to find food and shelter.

During the winter, Birds flock together and fly south in search of warmth and sustenance, where the insects can provide them food for a happy survival.

Betty, the Bird, shared her life with a partner, but sometimes her partner had to travel far away in order to find food like earthworms in rivers or fruits in the jungle. In the jungle, there was a man named 'The Griot'; he was the protractor of the news – like in Europe we learn the news through newspapers, radio or TV.

However, in the jungle, The Griot walked around the villages and talked to the people about the latest news. He was a very rich man, not in money or goods, but in knowledge. The history of the jungle was told by this man. The Griot knew Betty and her partner, who, during the rainy season, loved to fly together around the lush canopies of Virunga Park. One day, as The Griot was doing his usual walk around midday, he found himself tired and so sat on a tree trunk next to the road. Betty saw The Griot and flew down to him; she offered him a brown Caterpillar that she had collected from a palm tree. The rainforest was rich with palm trees, which harbour palm oil in the nuts and wine from their sap, then after death, provide perfect conditions for Caterpillars to thrive. The brown Caterpillar was a special gift as he was deliciously raw, as opposed to his bigger, white counterpart which must be fried before enjoying. Shortly after The Griot graciously accepted Betty's offer, he listened to her as she relayed a dire problem.

Betty and her partner loved the jungle; however, her partner was sometimes forced to fly far away in search of food, and they usually ate the Caterpillars which could be found on palm tree trunks. Betty had recently found a particular trunk which harboured a great number of these Caterpillars right in the jungle; this had excited her with the hope of an easier life with her partner, where he would no longer have to leave her behind to find food. So, Betty returned to the trunk a week later, only to find a huntsman collecting all of the Caterpillars. Betty fluttered down next to him and asked, "Why are you taking all of the Caterpillars?"

To which the Huntsman replied, "They are to feed my kids."

At this, Betty attempted to convince the man not to take them all, explaining that she needed some to feed her own family.

"Why should I share with a Bird?" the huntsman scoffed.

"Shame on you, bushman. You came to the jungle to hunt and now you are taking all the Caterpillars to feed your kids!"

The huntsman reacted furiously, throwing his machete at Betty, who swooped down to narrowly avoid the blade.

"You're lucky I don't have a gun, or else I would've killed you and had a barbecue for my kids!"

"Shame on you," Betty repeated and flew away.

The rule of the jungle was that all that grew in the bush, belonged to everybody, and everybody must share. Nevertheless, some malicious people, like the huntsman, tried to hide the food they found so that nobody else could share it.

The Griot was deeply disappointed with the huntsman's behaviour and advised Betty to go and visit the Chief. Therefore, the two of them began to make their way to the Chief's hut. Around Virunga Park, many of the indigenous people moved far away because animals such as Monkeys, Leopards and Elephants ate off their corps or killed their domestic animals.

When the pair arrived, the Chief was seated on the floor of his hut, talking about business with the elders. He wore a Leopard skin hat and held a large stick, symbolising his power. The Griot came forward and introduced Betty, who repeated her concern to the men. However, as she spoke, it seemed that the Chief was no longer listening; he had dozed off and an elder was nudging his side to wake him.

"Wake up!"

To which the Chief replied, "I am like a Leopard; when I am dozing, my eyes are closed but my ears are listening. Exactly like a Leopard; when he is dozing, his tail is still up." After hearing Betty, the Chief explained that he could not decide what to do before speaking with the hunter.

One of the elders turned to Betty and asked, "Who is the hunter you speak of?"

To which The Griot described the dark looks of the huntsman before the pair made their way back. While they walked through the thick jungle on the horizon, Betty was disheartened that the Chief didn't appear to be listening; she was offended by his behaviour and the way he slept while Betty tried to explain her problem after she had journeyed all the way to consult him. The Griot gravely listened and solemnly suggested to Betty that perhaps the Chief had been unlucky enough to have had some kind of illness transmitted from a mosquito.

A few days passed with no news. However, one morning Betty woke up to find that the Chief had called her to tell her that he himself could not find a suitable solution to the problem, and advised her to consult the king of the animals, and that perhaps he could do something for her.

The Griot explained to Betty, "Some forget that we are here in Virunga Park, where both human beings and animals are trying to survive in the same way."

The Chief had found out that the huntsman was found to be a close friend of one of the elders, and when confronted about the issue, he had argued that Betty had insulted him and convinced the elders not to pursue a trial.

This left Betty in a bad position; the Chief had refused to help her. She was but a tiny Bird in a jungle full of more powerful creatures – what hope did she have to be listened to? She sat heavy with disappointment.

The Griot looked at her and smiled, "Betty, you must remember, you are a beautiful part of nature. Your singing wakes the jungle in the morning, informs us that the sun is rising."

The next morning, The Griot rose very early and made his way to the huntsman's house, and sang like a Bird,

"Leave the Bird to live on Caterpillars,
She doesn't offend anyone.
In the evening when she flies,

She is dancing in the sky,
To express the joys of life.
In the morning, her cries tell us the sun will rise,
So, why force her not to feed,
Be reasonable human being,
For respect is reciprocal…"

For a long time, the animals had accepted the Lion as King of the animals, his stature and power gave him a great authority. For this reason, many sought his wisdom to resolve predicaments within the jungle.

However, when it came to disobedience, he was ruthless, which was why Betty hoped that he could help her. The huntsman had broken one of the vital rules of respect in the jungle. The selfishness expressed by men such as him was destroying the well-balanced relationship between men and animals in the jungle, where they shared the land in peace.

The journey to the King was arduous; Betty and The Griot had to make their way through the thickly forested jungle, all the way to the grassy savannah region. Along the way, other animals heard of Betty's story and decided to accompany them, despite the long trek away from their own homes. Chimpanzees, Monkeys and even some Elephants stood side by side with Betty and The Griot. They too had experienced the selfishness of men who harvested the fruits in the trees, leaving nothing for the animals but leaves.

The Griot was used to roaming long distances with his stick and Betty too often travelled far for food. However, many of the other animals struggled to keep pace with each other. After some distance, a Hyena spotted the unusual group and asked them where they were going. Upon hearing, The Griot explained that they were headed to see the Lion.

The Hyena was overcome with a sensation of fear. "You shall be killed!" he exclaimed.

However, The Griot calmly assured him that they came solely to restore peace to the jungle and thus the fear, which formerly encompassed the Hyena, subsided and he was gripped with curiosity, so he decided to walk amongst the other animals between The Griot, who strode far in front, and the Elephants, who steadily held the rear.

The jungle was quiet and the only sounds were of the distant cries of Monkeys and Birds. Leaves from the immense trees littered the ground and muffled the sounds of their walking. The Griot advised the group to eat whatever fruits they could find as they walked. He himself gathered some and sipped from a cold-water bottle. Man and animal walked together, in an Eden where all creatures stood side by side in harmony. Suddenly, a noise broke the silence, much like how the indigenous men did when working in the fields, to prevent the feeling of fatigue. The Griot began to sing:

"We are people of the jungle, We're not afraid of anything,
The massive jungle belongs to us,
Let us go boys,
Breathe the fresh air of the forest
Let's go boys,
Walking with pride because the jungle belongs to us."

At that moment, there was a thunderous clash of branches and a deafening roar cut through the still air. The group was frozen as a huge cat emerged from the foliage in front of them and seconds later, the animals fell into chaos, the Monkeys sprang up trees, the Elephants trumpeted and the others wailed in fear. However, the cat growled with authority and all fell silent.

"What is all this noise? You are disturbing my sleep; I have been hunting all night and then you bastards come and disregard any respect for stillness in this forest!" At the sight of the cat, The Griot laid down his machete.

"We are not bastards. We want no trouble and no fight. We would just like to be on our way."

At the impressive sight of The Griot's gallant stance facing the cat, the Monkeys began to climb down from their hiding places to stand by their leader. Slowly, the big cat's stand began to falter as the masses of animals defied their normal instincts and armed a united opposition. The Griot did not take up his weapon but calmly requested the cat to return to his lair peacefully and let the issue rest. After a long aggressive look at one of the Chimpanzees, the big cat stepped aside, but not before muttering,

"If this man was not here, I would've dealt with you one by one. Then you would never disturb my sleep again." After which, he skulked away.

Betty was flying high overhead, she looked down and could not make out where her friends were walking, due to the dense vegetation of the forest; however, as she lowered herself to locate the others, she flew past the large cat. Hastily, she sped between the trees and united with the group.

"Are you okay?" she asked, nervous to see if anyone had been hurt.

"We are fine." The Griot smiled, "we just met a new friend."

"A friend?" snapped the other animals as they clambered back from their hiding places.

The animals continued in silence, shaken by the event which had taken place but Betty had found the amusing side.

"Wow, even with all of you together, one big cat has frightened you this much?" She scoffed and swooped down to rest on the Elephant's back.

"You have wings, so you can fly away – you do not have to face this kind of danger," the Elephant replied, to which the Hyena added,

"This is true! You are the only one in full safety. If I had wings like you, I'd never have to worry about dying of hunger, I would find food all the time."

However, the Monkeys heard this and erupted with cackling, commenting on the fact that the Hyena was just a scavenger, who strutted around aggressively, snatching food from those who had laboured so hard to hunt it. The Hyenas were the reason that Leopards learned to hide their prey up in trees to gain some peace. The Hyena couldn't argue but simply retaliated by claiming that the Monkeys were cowards as they hid in the trees all day, too scared to confront the big, bad world on the ground. Then, smarmily, the Hyena turned to the Monkeys,

"Where we are going, there are no trees, only the Savannah. What will you do in the face of danger?"

"They will bite the dust!" chuckled the Elephant. However, in that moment, The Griot shot them a look which commanded them to leave the issue and walk in peace.

"You must watch how you speak, be respectful. This kind of language would be disgraceful and disrespectful in front of the king. You must think how a wise man thinks."

"I think a wise man would give us all the bananas!" jabbed a Monkey, and the others burst out with a rumbling laughter.

"All you think about is food, I'm sure you'd want something else from the king," sniggered the Elephant.

"Okay," the Monkey retorted, "I should ask the king why he has such a hairy neck –"

"You most certainly would not!" interrupted The Griot.

And thus, the animals trotted on, past the borders of the bushy Virunga Park and into the dry Savannah of Serengeti Park.

To reach the king's throne, one had to pass through the Lions' territory only with special permission. One had to wait on the threshold until they were met with a guide Lion. If one was to simply 'walk through', he would be ripped apart by the pride.

The group was silent as a bronze-coloured Lioness escorted them, without a word, through the pride land towards the king. The king sat shrouded by Lionesses and a wide perimeter, where strong male Lions were posted, each one with their ferocious black eyes fixed upon every blink and twitch of the animals. The king's gold-herculean body had not faded with age but looked as if a fierce fire surged rampant about his face and neck. However, he gently turned his great head towards the animals and in a low thunder asked what the purpose of their visit was.

The guide retorted that they came in peace and for his help. The Griot expanded by explaining the nature of Betty's issue and that they believed since he was the king of all animals, he could help them. There was a pause.

Then The king and all of the pride erupted in a chorus of laughter.

"You came to me because some humans were eating insects?" he looked at the Monkeys and Chimpanzees, "how do you feed yourselves?"

"Fruits and bananas," they murmured. The king looked puzzled, he did not know what a banana was, a problem that The Griot quickly cleared up. The king's great head cocked in confusion; he had not known any other diet than meat.

"And what do you eat, Gorilla?" to which The Griot replied that he ate leaves, grass, shoots and fruits too. At this, the king raised his huge body up with a smile, he looked out from the top of the hill upon which they were gathered, gazing at the many animals grazing across the grassy savannah. The view of Serengeti offered herds of Zebra, Antelope and Buffalo. The picture warmed the king's heart and filled him with pride, he turned to his peers and said, "It is not by accident that I am king of the animals. How could a king be fed by leaves of a tree, or by grass, or by fruits? Every day, I eat fresh meat, brought to me either by my wives or soldiers." He paced back towards the cloud of Lionesses.

"These are my wives, who will eventually be swapped for younger Lionesses and these wives will be gifted to the soldiers who stand guard behind you." He surveyed the cowering faces of all animals who patiently awaited his verdict.

He stood up and stepped towards them. "Why are you still here?"

"You didn't answer Betty's query." The Griot solemnly replied. To which the Lion laughingly said, "My dear friends, I can't do anything for you; if the humans are eating the insects – it's a pleasure for me because it means that they aren't eating my meat. Also, if other animals are feeding on fruits and grass and not eating living creatures, is that not better for nature?" to which the soldiers gave nods of agreement.

Betty, perched on a bare branch, cried, "What about me then?"

The King laughed again, asking his soldiers, "Oh, what can we do for this poor Bird?"

To which one soldier grunted, "We have no time to spend on a Bird. Maybe she should go find some nice humans to confide in –" he gestured to The Griot, "– like him!" At this point, the wide circle of soldiers was thunderous with laughter.

"Well, that's it then," growled the king.

"I am sorry, I can't do anything for you. In fact, I hope very much that the humans continue eating the insects and not my meat."

The king ordered two of his soldiers to accompany his guests back to the border of the savannah. Promptly, The Griot took the lead and the others followed him. The two soldiers silently dropped back, they had planned to have words with the Hyena, who trod near the rear of the pack.

As they approached the Hyena, he became frightened. However, they hushed that he shouldn't panic.

"We are your friends," they sneered, "we want only to speak with you."

"What do you want?" The Hyena's eyes were wild with fear.

"We have a business proposition for you, but this must remain a secret between us."

"What business?" his face fixed upon the ground, wondering what terrifying proposition would be uttered. The soldiers described how they had always been curious about the taste of Monkey. On hearing this, the Hyena let out a startled yelp.

"Shh, shh. You will attract attention to us," the soldiers hissed through gnarled ivory teeth.

"You don't want me to…kill a Monkey, do you?" the shocked Hyena replied in dismay,

"Not until you can confirm that this will remain a secret." The Hyena stared blankly at the two soldiers whose shoulders towered over his own. "Look, when you arrive back at the bush, try to convince one or two Monkeys to follow you to where we are going to leave you and your friends. Tell them you found a garden heavy with fruit at the border of the savannah. Once you deliver them, we will finish the job."

The Hyena nodded, digesting the information, "And you'll kill them. What do I get?"

"We will deliver you some fresh Zebra meat; we know how much you Hyenas like it. It will be enough to feed you and your family."

The idea was seductive, and when the Hyena returned home to his contemporaries, he explained the situation how the Monkeys had humiliated him repeatedly, entertaining the idea of a sweet revenge.

However, as he spoke, an elderly Hyena was listening, he explained to the youngers, "I have made many deals in my life. However, I have never made a deal with someone who is stronger than myself. What will stop them from eating you after the deal is done? I advise you to maintain business with animals like Antelopes or Zebras. In that case, if the deal goes wrong, you are able to defend yourself. Also, don't forget that Monkeys are very wise." The others nodded with agreement, urging him to pass on the deal for it was far too risky.

In the pride lands, the soldiers strutted back to the king with arrogance. They spread the word that they would be bringing a special gift to the pride, upon which, the Lions became very curious. The king rose with intrigue.

"What kind of meat do you mean?" he called, to which the soldiers replied,

"Monkey meat!" This caused an uproar of excitement, no Lion, not even the king, had experienced the meat of a Monkey before.

"Oh, king, you wait and see, we have a deal, a commercial exchange…we will trade Zebra meat with our new partner, for Monkeys…" The air of shock evolved into one of scepticism among the pride.

However, when the time came for the Lions to meet at the agreed place and to receive the Monkeys, there was no sign of the Hyena. They waited until they were tired, only a few Birds flew overhead, as if to mock them.

The indigenous had a saying very suited to the moment that those Lions had experienced: 'Wait and wait again, like the Chimpanzee who awaits a tail from God'. This proverb came from the pondering of a group of frustrated Chimpanzees, who wondered why the other Monkeys had been gifted with long tails and they had not.

An old Tortoise had told them about the way their ancestors were certain that God had been exhausted at the time of their creation and that he would one day return to attach their tails. But the Chimpanzees never understood that they were created as they were – without a tail, like the Lions who returned home, tired and never having tasted Monkey meat. There began the animosity between the Lions and the Hyenas, as the Lions decided they would take revenge on that Hyena.

On their way back, Betty adopted her usual habit of flying ahead to scout for danger. However, after she came back, she told the others that she had to leave them and go somewhere else.

"Why?" The general outcry rose from the group. Betty explained,

"I've just seen an area full of crickets!" This discovery corresponded with the special time of year in Virunga and Serengeti, when the crickets and grasshoppers descended upon the region. The Monkeys asked what on Earth she could do with all those crickets.

"It is for a good cause," replied Betty, "I am going to fill my bags with them and take them to as many Birds' nests as possible so the babies can eat." Without time for opposition, Betty took flight, the others remained somewhat stupefied by the loss of Betty and watched her silhouette disappear into the sky. The Griot assumed his usual leadership and began walking the route home.

After a few days of quiet trekking, the group made it back home. Disheartened by the rejection and disinterest of the king. The realisation came over them all that their identity as herbivores and omnivores, held them back from fair treatment in the kingdom.

On Sunday, twice a month, the priest came to a rustic hut with four wooden pillars and dusted with straw situated in the village square. This was where many of the indigenous people met to reconnect and worship, as majority of them were Christians.

The following Sunday, among the faithful church-goers, sat the huntsman and the Chief elders, singing at full belt, their love for the Lord. As Betty flew nearby the hut, she heard this noise and decided to find out what was going on. As she descended towards to noise, she recognised that The Griot was also seated among the congregation. She was astonished at the way the natives so passionately asked the Lord for help with their everyday lives. Then she saw the huntsman leap from his seat, dancing and singing for the Lord.

After the worship was finished, the people greeted the priest on their way out of the church, some of them asking him to lay hands on them. She watched as the huntsman appeared to approach the priest for this same blessing, however, she quickly intervened,

"You came for the blessing?" she directed at the huntsman, who spun around, surprised.

"What is this silly Bird doing here? Animals don't come in this church, especially not Birds like you!"

Betty turned to the priest, "This man tried to kill me and has stolen all of my food."

At this point, a crowd began to gather. The Chief elders snarled, "Looks like this Bird has come to disturb us all again."

However, the huntsman was frozen where he stood. The priest asked Betty to explain. She told him the whole story. After she had finished, the crowd turned on the huntsman, shocked that he had the nerve to implore the Lord's blessing.

One villager, who had been following the conversation, asked the huntsman to show everyone where the Caterpillar-filled tree trunk was, so that he could share it with all of the others.

However, the priest advised the huntsman, and to all those listening that, "The ideology of Virunga Park is to consider everybody, whether it is a man or an animal. Both have the same rights in this land."

This elicited much murmuring from the crowd, yet the priest continued, he stepped forward, commanding that the huntsman to allow Betty to access an equal share of the Caterpillars or else he would be considered a thief. Many shouted in objection, claiming that they too should be allowed to have the Caterpillars. Some shouted about what the fate of the elders and the huntsman should be, others commented that they had seen the huntsman's wife selling the Caterpillars in the market. The huntsman and the elders raised their hands behind their heads with a final comment, "What is this Bird's problem, always looking for trouble? Can't she for once forget this damn issue?"

After this turn of events, The Griot went around the park, spreading the news, singing,

"Shame of the huntsman,
He hid the trunk of Caterpillars to feed only his family,
Today, he is considered a thief,
This man cannot share,
The Bird finally gets justice from the man."

As he was walking, The Griot came across his old Monkey friends who jumped from tree to tree. They asked The Griot what had happened, to which he replied, "Life is like the jawbone of a Goat."

The Monkeys looked at each other, baffled.

So, The Griot continued,

"When human eats his food, he chews it between his teeth by moving them up and down. However, when a Goat chews his grass, the jawbone moves left to right and right to left. If life is like the jawbone of a Goat, it simply means that the history of life is repetitive. The problem that appeared today had appeared a long time ago, but human beings just don't learn. They continue to be selfish and bring shame to their life…"

The Monkeys followed the tale with their black eyes.

"…Just like the huntsman." One of them continued The Griot's speech. The Griot smiled at their understanding before he resumed walking and singing,

"Right to left and left to right,
Like the jawbone of a Goat!"

As he left, the Monkeys started cackling at The Griot, "Here is a man, making fun of men!"

And with that notion, they continued soaring back into the treetops, jumping from tree tops, left to right and right to left, like the jawbone of a Goat.

Chapter 2

Queen Makoso, the Strong Female Rhino

As we know, Betty was a single female who lived alone. In Virunga Park, there were just two seasons; the rainy season and the dry season. During these dry seasons, many of the insects that the Birds relied on, become scarce. One day, in the midst of a particularly dry season, after telling her he was fed up with the insects that they were eating, her partner took off faraway in search of better food and never returned.

After the problems regarding the hunter had settled down, Betty returned to the bush to collect Caterpillars from the palm tree. On her way back home, she felt so lonely and began singing to herself, "I am a single woman, still hoping one day I will meet my prince charming…" Betty wore two rings on her feet, one for her and one representing her prince charming. She loved children, often collecting extra Caterpillars as gifts for her friend's baby,

"…I am a single woman
Still waiting for prince charming
The day I meet him, I will offer him a ring
The rain will dampen my skin but not my heart;
Never search for love,
Wait and love will come to you
Then you will taste the sweetness of love."

A male Rhinoceros overheard Betty's singing and shouted to her, "I love you, Betty, you sweet Bird!"

However, this declaration quickly elicited a vicious reaction from his partner, Makoso, "Why are you appreciating other females when I am right here with you!" This quickly escalated into a substantial fight, which ended with Makoso beating the male to the floor while he called for help. All the nearby inhabitants of Virunga Park heard his cries and swiftly began running to help the victim, not knowing what they were going to find. Many presumed there was a thief or an intruder within the park, but all were startled with what they discovered – Makoso standing above the male and beating him. The Chimpanzee was distressed; usually, the males were the dominant figure in relationships, and he was awestruck by the strength of this female. The two Rhinoceros were separated while the others digested what they had just encountered.

The news spread quickly through the village and many males, like the Chimpanzee, were baffled by this female's ability to beat up her partner! This had never happened before in Virunga Park, with the exception of the female tiger. The Griot told all about Makoso, "The strong female Rhinoceros, who was the only daughter of the old Rhinoceros king, Boma Rhino. Boma Rhino was incredibly strong and no other male Rhino could challenge him. He had a huge plot full of sweet potatoes and cannabis leaves. These leaves could grow anywhere in the jungle, however, only the humans highly desired them as they felt the leaves transported them to heaven while they smoked them. There are two things a man cannot avoid: drinking and smoking. The villagers got their alcohol from the palm trees and smoked cannabis until foreigners introduced tobacco. Despite the demand, Boma wouldn't let the villagers collect any off his property. The villagers would often rob his plot while Boma was asleep, until one day, Boma caught and killed one of the thieves on his land, assuming that they were there to steal his sweet potatoes. The news of the killing spread, creating a deep, growing animosity within the villagers towards the king. For this reason, Boma was shot with a poison arrow by them."

The Griot told his friends that, "A long time ago, the government had proposed to build a hospital in the village, which meant that the sick would not have to travel far away for treatment. However, the people of the village refused this proposition and requested, instead, to have a brewery built. The villagers already had witchcraft and healers whom they had been accustomed to for years, some tried to convince the others of the benefits of a hospital, yet the villagers argued that, ultimately, the hospitals would not stop death. It was a common view to enjoy what life you are given and drink lots of palm-wine!"

Therefore, the hospital was never built. Instead, many palm trees were planted in order to produce more of this wine. In this instance, the Chimpanzees and Monkeys all agreed with the villagers that a hospital would be a terrible place.

They agreed that if you were sick, it was better that the doctor comes to visit you in the comfort of your own home. The Elephants criticised the humans for the idea as they argued that the humans just created unnecessary places to rest.

This viewpoint arose from the fact that the Elephant was an animal which remained standing throughout his life; it was very rare that an Elephant relaxed.

The Elephants predicted that if the humans needed so much rest, they must be very tired. In which case, the humans should drink clean water and live a quiet and pleasurable life.

Returning to the point, when Boma was alive, only he and the brave soldiers ate sweet potatoes, while only grass and herbs were reserved for the women and children. Those women had the role of producing young and nurturing the herd. However, when Boma died, Makoso, who was already big for her age, decided to continue the reign of her father. She said,

"If anyone wants to contest my authority, they can fight me for it." And unbelievably, she defeated every soldier who challenged her. From that day, Makoso continued to reign as 'Queen of the Rhinos', inherited her father's plot and ate sweet potatoes with the strong soldiers every day.

This law regarding food being reserved for the men was not only evident in the animal kingdom but also seen in the villagers, who did not permit the women and children to eat Tortoise meat. This was because the Tortoise was believed to be a very wise animal who lived a life longer than 100 years. This wisdom was believed to be carried into whoever eats it, and those who did eat it wished for their lives to be long like that of the Tortoise as well. Similarly, consuming Leopard's meat was in the hope of inheriting bravery. Other meats included snakes, Crocodiles and Gorilla, which were only to be cooked and consumed by men. However, some women, such as the Chief's wives or rich women broke this tradition at times, yet not without the other villagers, as a result, fearing them.

"Beware of those women…" People would mutter, "– they have tasted the sacred meats." The villagers, therefore, believed that those women had inherited the masculine traits of strength, cunning and intelligence and they would be avoided and remain unmarried.

This came from the patriarchal culture which portrayed women as inferior to men, they didn't have any of the same rights or roles; they simply lived under the power of men. Therefore, Makoso's reversal of this dynamic showed just how strong she was.

It was this strength which made the other male Rhinos warn her husband against marrying Makoso, as they foresaw this kind of beating and the husband's consequent shame and emasculation.

As the days passed, the male Rhino and his wife lived a peaceful life. One morning, an Antelope was chomping at the grass nearby the Rhino's plot, although he was enjoying his grass, he noticed the Rhino's wife was eating something very different. The Antelope wanted to consult with the Rhino about it but was terrified to approach such a juggernaut of an animal. After a long night of thinking, the Antelope returned to the same place the next day to meet with the Rhino. The Antelope filled himself with a few deep breaths of courage and approached him, despite a polite greeting the Rhino did not respond; he only stared back warily at the Antelope. Yet, the Antelope continued,

"Why are you always alone? Why don't you have any children by now to be helping you out?"

The Rhino scoffed and replied that he had no children but that he was doing fine by himself.

To which the Antelope continued, "But it is a very long life to live alone with your partner. You must know Makoso will never give you children…"

The Rhino interrupted, "How do you know, you silly animal! My wife simply isn't interested in children but I trust that one day she will give me one."

"My God! You are dreaming. It will never happen!"

"How do you know?"

"Everyone knows. You wife will never be able to conceive because she has male hormones."

The Rhino was shocked and outraged by the Antelope's bravery, "Who told you this stupidity?"

To which the Antelope calmly replied, "Just look at the power she has. She carries male hormones in her body! On the outside, she looks like a woman but inside, she is the same as the other soldiers. If I were you, I would go and get an actual girlfriend. Many girls would love to be with you and you are killing yourself by being so lonely all the time."

The Rhino was wounded harshly by this comment, but he continued to graze grass silently. "I know some lovely young beautiful Rhinos; I could introduce you to them." The Antelope suggested, to which the Rhino quietly agreed. After a while, the Rhino had been dating one of the girls that the Antelope had introduced him to. One day, the Antelope returned to pay a visit to the Rhino, requesting that he receive 5 kilograms of sweet potatoes. However, the Rhino refused, retorting that he was not just some charity who gives away sweet potatoes to people. Yet the Antelope smiled and replied,

"You are like grease which, right now, is in a refrigerator as it is hard and cold – but when grease is put in the heat, it disappears. Think long and hard before I expose you to your wife regarding your lovely young friend. Give me the potatoes."

Faced with this, the Rhino gave the Antelope what he wanted but told him sternly not to return again. To which the Antelope disagreed, "Now we have an agreement, you and I. Whenever I need potatoes, sir, you must comply with my request." The Rhino looked up to the sky, realising the trap he had walked into. The Antelope left, greatly satisfied by his malicious work, now he could consume the food of royalty.

Back in his own territory, the Antelope and his friend, the Buffalo, were sharing a great portion of sweet potatoes. In this kingdom, one must be cunning, like the Antelope was, in order to live a pampered life. The Buffalo was taken aback by the way in which the Antelope, a weaker animal was able to retrieve such rich foods, consequently deciding to stick by his side a little closer and find out his secret.

Some months later, the young female Rhino, who had become pregnant, gave birth to a baby boy Rhino. However, the male Rhino avoided her and only visited his son very scarcely. For this reason, the young mum lost her patience and decided that she would meet with Queen Makoso herself and reveal her husband's secret. When she arrived before Queen Makoso, she found that, due to the shame of Makoso's beatings, the male Rhino had run away from the kingdom. Despite this, Makoso welcomed the poor young mum into her kingdom and adopted the baby boy. The rest is history, with Makoso delighted to have an heir.

The Antelope searched everywhere for the male Rhino, with the hope to renegotiate a deal for his sweet potatoes, but never found him.

Chapter 3
Leopard: Trickery Animal

The Leopard was a very tricky and aggressive animal, especially when it was hungry.

The Leopards caused many problems for the villagers, mostly the hunters.

When a hunter killed an animal in order to feed his family, it was ill-advised to confront a Leopard on his way. With their highly developed sense of smell, Leopards could quickly detect the smell of game and if they found this game, they would never let the hunter go. The paradox was that the Leopards would not eat human flesh; he simply wanted the hunter's catch.

One day, a hunter named Dr Bertrand discovered a place where Monkeys gathered to eat fruits. This place was similar to a mango tree plantation, which was also flooded with other fruits and flowers. As was a well-known fact at the time, the villagers enjoyed the flesh of Monkeys for their breakfast. For this reason, Bertrand was delighted to have found this little haven. He thought of the way the villagers prepared the Monkey's flesh, by roasting it and boiling it in salt water to remove the hair. This feast was justified by the well-known saying 'He who starts well, finishes well'. Therefore, as a hunter, he felt he must supply this Monkey meat.

On that day, Bertrand found the place buzzing with Monkeys who had flocked to taste the sweet fruits. He walked very slowly, careful not to be spotted, holding a locally manufactured rifle at his hip. Believing that he was completely unseen, he gently advanced towards the Monkeys, however, a Leopard spotted him, who was attracted by the sound of the Monkeys. The Leopard himself had much skill in catching Monkeys, he would lurk in the underbrush while the Monkeys played at the top of trees like children, waiting for one to make a grave error and drop fruit onto the floor. Then, as the Monkey would swing down to collect it, the Leopard would not miss his prey.

This time, the Leopard understood that he was not alone in this hunt for Monkeys, he was up against a man with a gun. This meant that the hunter could kill much more effortlessly, for this reason, the Leopard, as malicious as he was, preferred to hide and follow the hunter until he killed a Monkey.

During his stalking, Bertrand killed three Monkeys and put them in his game-bag. Although he had a gun, the locally made guns could only kill small animals like Monkeys and Birds as the bullets were so small. Therefore, the hunter would always leave the larger animals in peace, and that was the principle of the jungle. Bertrand, after killing his Monkeys, began to return home, dreaming of his breakfast with his wife and friends. After around fifty yards, the Leopard appeared behind him and threw him to the ground with a brutal blow. The rifle fell a few feet from Bertrand, with the Leopard standing in between. Bertrand shuffled back, wishing to escape, but the Leopard ripped off his game-bag and snatched two of the Monkeys before running off into the distance. He got up, picked up his game-bag, almost forgetting to collect his fallen rifle and staggered away. This was a catastrophe for Bertrand. He began to feel nauseous at being robbed defencelessly, having the food taken from his mouth. It was as if a worker had worked for a whole month and had his pay stolen. Bertrand began to think how he would explain this misfortune to his family and friends on his way home.

The next time Bertrand went hunting, he went accompanied by one of his fellow hunters. A selfishness lives within the hunters, they like to hunt alone and not share their prey amongst others. When Bertrand had discovered the location where the Monkeys thrived in great numbers, he told nobody.

However, the Leopard's attack changed his mind.

This time, he rejoiced in the company of his friend, hoping that together, they could avoid another misadventure. That day, the two hunters killed eight Monkeys, while the Leopard watched. He watched how the hunter caught and killed the Monkeys before putting them in their bags. The Leopard left the hunters to continue, content in the decision to hunt other animals. Thinking deeply, he turned to his friend, the cat. The cat was also a very crafty and intelligent animal who was widely considered as the little brother of the Leopards. The cat would live with the Leopards, feeding them inside information about the lives of the villagers from their time as domesticated animals. The cat spoke positively to the Leopard,

"It's no problem if there are two hunters. I know their type well; I live with hunters like them." With that, the Leopard and the cat assumed their usual habit of waiting for the hunters to begin walking back with their full game-bags. The two hunters started to return, trustful of their safety due to their greater united force. Suddenly, they heard the noise of an animal ahead, stepping back quickly, they shielded their game-bags and listened to locate the noise. After that, the hunters heard disturbances behind them making them start forward again, before halting as the animal cries arose again from ahead.

The hunters began to panic, feeling surrounded by unknown danger. Bertrand's companion suggested that it was better to back away towards the disturbances rather than continue towards the wild animal cries ahead. At that moment, they turned their backs, which was all the time the Leopard needed to leap with an incredible ferocity, which knocked both hunters to the floor. As the hunters scrambled on the floor, the Leopard ripped open their game-bags before disappearing into the bush.

***

The villagers were all afraid to leave their homes during the night due to a long history of suspicion surrounding a mysterious phantom. The nights were silent, only adorned by the whistling of nocturnal insects and crickets, however, predators like Leopards and cats patrolled the area, like sharks in the water, looking for victims. As a result of the Leopard's behaviour, the Chiefs agreed to offer the Leopard work in order to prevent further attacks on hunters. The work they offered could be described as 'animal security' in the abattoir, where many stray Dogs wandered the ground scavenging for waste-meat. As these Dogs grew in number, the situation began to be intolerable, and the Chief decided that the Leopard could patrol the abattoir and control the surge of Dogs. The Leopard happily wore the animal security badge and began to drive away the Dogs from the slaughterhouse. The stray Dogs were terrified of the Leopards, knowing that they could be killed without a second breath, realising their hopelessness, they found the occurrence very hard to accept. It was this dumping ground, where most of them found their staple diet and now the Leopard was between them and their food. The Dogs came together to discuss a solution. In that meeting, one suggested that they cooperate with the Leopard; however, taming an animal like a Leopard was nearly impossible.

"Let's send him a beautiful female Dog who can distract and charm him, thereby leaving us a way into the abattoir without being seen."

The following night, the Dogs put this plan in motion. At first, when the female approached the Leopard, he agreed to cooperate with her, however, after a while he turned to her and stated, "If we end up arguing, we won't get very far. I have no doubt you will be my first taste of Dog meat." Upon hearing this, the female ran away quicker than she had ever ran in her life.

The Leopard found the scrap meat on the dump inedible and wondered how the Dogs could be nourished on the refuse. As the Leopard watched the Dogs from where he was sitting, he asked himself why these Dogs did not hunt in the bush for proper meat. The Leopard cherished the tastes of fresh quality meat, especially when he had just killed it. To him, the Dogs were disgusting swines with no concept of hygiene.

The Leopard warned the Dogs not to approach him again due to their filthiness, on which the Dogs were very upset, not only were they offended by his comments but also devastated that their efforts to collaborate with the Leopard had failed.

The Dogs gathered again to discuss their new position when one had an evil idea. One of the Dogs suggested planting inflated cushions under where the Leopard goes to rest, that way every time he moved, the natives would think that the Leopard was just farting all the time. This would ruin the Leopard's reputation and the natives would fire him for being rude and dirty.

The Dogs got to work and made the pillow very early the following morning, concealing it under the Leopard's seat. The Dogs watched and laughed as the pillow let out gross noises with the Leopard's every move, attracting negative attention from the female villagers who sat in the nearby reception. The women became disgusted by the Leopard's disrespect and reported what they thought was rude behaviour to his boss. The same occurred the following day, after which the Leopard apologised to the women, explaining he had no idea where the noises were coming from. However, his repetitive actions eventually elicited a visit from the owner to the Leopard. The owner demanded that the Leopard change his lewd behaviour or be sacked.

From that day onwards, the Leopard never again sat in that chair after apologising repeatedly to the owner. One morning, the owner had received a visit from a customer, he spoke with him in front of the abattoir reception, the customer asked to be seated and, after looking around for good seating, the owner saw the Leopard's seat. As the owner lowered himself into the seat, to everyone's surprise, the armchair emitted a terrible sound as if he had just let out a massive fart! He immediately shot up out of the chair and stared at it in disbelief, stating to everyone watching that he had no gas.

The women at reception were astonished, as this must have been what had been happening to the Leopard. After this embarrassing situation, the owner decided to get rid of the chair, regretting his chastisement of the Leopard. After apologising profusely to the Leopard, they became good friends, which meant that the Dogs' plan had backfired horribly.

Now the Leopard had the full confidence of the owner, who, one day, had to leave to attend an event in another village far from the abattoir. He planned to bring some animals to the event, so he asked the Leopard if he could escort two bulls to the event for him. The Leopard did not refuse this request and thus walked behind the two bulls in single file, they walked this way for many hours.

However, during the course of the road, they met with a group of Hyenas, who had just returned from an unsuccessful hunting trip and were consequently very hungry. Upon seeing the two bulls, they realised that this meeting could be a wonderful opportunity; however, challenging the Leopard would be pointless, and their best option would be to attempt to charm him. The Hyenas approached the Leopard, enquiring to where he was going with all that food, complimenting him on the health of the bulls. The Leopard sternly replied that the bulls belonged to his boss and that he was escorting them to an auction in the other village.

The Hyenas continued to inform the Leopard about their unsuccessful hunting expedition in Park Serengeti, commenting that then would be the best time to hunt in Park as there were a huge number of herbivores on the savannah. These words sunk deep into the Leopard's mind as he remembered the beautiful days that he spent hunting Antelope and Zebra in Park Serengeti.

The Leopard thought hard about returning to his homeland in Serengeti instead of living off the meat from the abattoir.

While the Leopard struggled with his conflicting loyalties, the Hyenas plotted a diversion in the road that would lead the bulls into the bush. The Hyenas killed both bulls, and after struggling, and failing, to finish all the meat began to think about a second plan because the men were waiting for the Leopard to deliver the bulls.

Before the owner began searching for them, they hid the remaining meat and carried the Leopard into the village themselves, claiming him to be dead. The Hyenas claimed to the distraught men that they had found him dying on the road, unlikely to survive, lying on a bed of palm leaves. This news spread through the town fast and even spread to the surrounding villages. The Hyenas placed a jaw of an animal carcass over the Leopard's head, and people and animals all flocked to see the body of the great Leopard, wondering what caused his sudden death? The Hyenas advised the Leopard not to breathe deeply when animals viewed his body, they also tied his tail down so as not to allow it to spring upright, as all Leopards' tails do. The Dogs arrived first to see the Leopard, his death was great news for them, and there were whispers among them of 'the executioner is dead!' The Dogs laughed and joked about the rotting teeth of the carcass, which caused anger to rise up in the Leopard, yet he managed to suppress this rage to keep up the facade.

When the news reached the owner, he was drinking with his friends, waiting for the Leopard to arrive. On hearing the news, he immediately rushed to see the corpse, not caring so much about the Leopard but about his two bulls.

Approaching the spot where the Leopard lay, he hadn't anticipated the huge number of animals that were gathered around him.

"Where are my bulls?" the owner shouted. Astonished, everyone turned to look at him. A Rhino had the courage to answer him,

"What bulls do you mean?" To which the owner explained that the Leopard was supposed to have been escorting two bulls to the town. All the spectators drew a blank, they had heard nothing about the bulls. The owner started bawling at the crowd about the whereabouts of these bulls. The owners' friend suggested that the Leopard might have sold the bulls; however, they found no money on the Leopard. After a little while of commotion, the owner looked down at the Leopard,

"You are making fun of me. Wake up. You wake up and give me my money or my bulls." Quickly, the Hyenas intervened to calm the owner. The Elephant told the owner to quit talking to a corpse; it would not wake up. "I know my money or my bulls are hidden somewhere!" he turned to his friend, "can you find me a whip?" His friend was startled, asking why he would need a whip, the owner replied, "I need to whip this stupid animal!" At this announcement, all of the crowd became riled up, they cried protests which explained that whipping a corpse was disgusting and unfair. "A robber or criminal must be punished before he is buried, that is our culture!" Shouted the owner over the angry crowd. The Hyenas quickly gathered around the Leopard, trying to calm the situation, the commotion had attracted the attention of another man who suggested to the owner,

"It is not worth whipping this animal, don't you know much his skin is worth? It doesn't matter whether he is buried or not, all that matters is that we use his skin, it is worth a fortune! All the Chiefs desire the skin of this great Leopard, it will more than cover the cost of your two bulls and we can share the money."

The owner appeared silenced, but wary of sharing any profits, so the man continued, "As it was my idea, I can locate a buyer for this skin." The owner nodded his head and mentioned that he knew of a Chief who may be interested. At this turn of events, the Hyenas looked at each other in horror.

Luckily, the Elephant argued that the animals should have the corpse there to observe for one last night before they skin him the following day. Thus, the owner returned home, leaving the animals to their former activities. The owner smiled all the way home with the thought of all the money he would get from skinning the great Leopard. The others eventually scattered and the Hyenas reassured them that they would guard the corpse overnight.

Late that night, when everyone was asleep, the Hyenas woke up the Leopard and informed him it was time to escape. The Leopard was exhausted and said he would never be a part of those silly games again. As he removed the old jaw carcass, he thought of those rude Dogs, stating that the next time he sees those Dogs, he would eat them in one piece. They rushed to leave the place; however, they did not see the Tortoise who stood only a few feet away, at seeing the group attempting to run away he shouted, "Leopard, you are not dead!" They jumped, terrified at this noise. Telling the Tortoise to shut his mouth, they threatened that if he was to alert anyone in the village, they would return to kill him. The Tortoise agreed not to reveal what he had seen, fearing for his life.

However, as he lay in his bed unable to sleep, he decided to tell this crazy story to The Griot early that morning.

When the morning broke, the Tortoise went straight to The Griot's home, he found The Griot in a frantic state, he rushed around his home, getting ready to leave.

"Where are you going on this early morning?" Asked the Tortoise.

"Did you not hear about the Leopard? As the protector of animals, I must stop this skinning!" At this, the Tortoise started to laugh, "What's funny?" The griot stared at the Tortoise. Then, the Tortoise explained the surreal events he had witnessed last night. The Griot found it hard to believe that the Leopard tricked everyone and that nobody actually checked to see if he was actually dead! However, The Griot was relieved that the Leopard was safe and free. The Tortoise added,

"From yesterday I knew something was wrong because the Leopard lay dead in the street but his only true friend, the cat, did not arrive to see his body." The Griot elaborated that the animals had intelligence which allowed them to foresee some obstacles, however, this intelligence was limited. They did not have the ability to analyse the future, which was one of the differences between animals and men. The Leopard could not do what he did alone, but now his life was in danger. The Griot expressed his concern that the Leopard would now be a prize for the men and would be targeted in hunting trips from now on, not only for revenge but also for his, now very valuable, skin. The Chiefs desired a Leopard, Lion or tiger skin to lay on the ground with the head intact, to symbolise power to their neighbours.

The Leopards often wondered why the men came into the park in order to find food instead of supplying it in their own village. To them, it was a violation of territory, which was why they believed they had the right to attack them. On the other hand, the Leopards also often attacked the villager's pets to warn them to stop disturbing their jungle.

For this reason, a Chief who dominated his opponents was regarded as a Leopard as they did not accept the presence of other individuals that challenge their authority.

Chapter 4

Sula Cointer, the Chimpanzee

Virunga Park created a haven of peace between every creature, with each animal living quietly in his corner, sharing the incredible vegetation. Amongst them, were groups of Chimpanzees who were peaceful herbivores, who thrived among the canopies of leaves and fruits and with a lack of predators, they appeared to be promised a bright future. Life for them was beautiful. Our friend, The Griot, often came to visit these Chimpanzees and shared stories with them, he told them all about what had been happening in the park and villages. Of all the stories they were told, one Chimpanzee became especially interested in the stories involving humans; how they live and their origin. This Chimpanzee, who went by the name of Sula Cointer, wanted to understand the nature of mankind, for example, why men walked on two limbs while the Chimpanzees still utilised all four. The Griot attempted to satisfy his curiosity by explaining that, according to scientists, humans had descended from Chimpanzees and that changes in their environment led to them eventually walking upright.

Upon hearing this information, Sula decided that he wished to live in the village instead and rectify himself so he could walk upright amongst the humans. Sula convinced himself that, if he was indeed the ancestor of the man, then he could successfully imitate his way of life. The Griot advised Sula that if he wished to give up life in the trees and walk amongst the men, he should definitely attempt to find some clothes, offering him some of his own breeches. Initially, Sula's cousins made fun of him, but they later began to feel jealous of the way Sula's relationship with the humans began to develop and so they too asked The Griot for some breeches.

The natives found the actions of these Chimpanzees immensely amusing and began to admire these young Chimpanzees.

One day, Sula and his cousins were walking around the village when they met a man who was wearing shoes. At this point, the Chimpanzees were wearing shirts and trousers that were given to them by the Chief. On seeing this man, they approached him with questions regarding the purpose of wearing shoes, however, the man refused to speak to them, ridiculing them and calling them animals. Sula followed him, insisting that they speak, even addressing him respectfully as 'Uncle'. The man was surprised and infuriated that this Chimpanzee called him 'Uncle'.

He turned around and said, "You are pathetic liars, stop trying to be something you are not!" he sneered and walked away.

After seeing this man wearing sandals, Sula found The Griot, and asked him if he could get him some of his own. Despite being a good man, The Griot feared that he would not find any sandals which could fit the feet of Chimpanzees, however, The Griot told Sula to follow him deep into the village where a shoemaker lived who created sandals from the tires of old vehicles. At the top of the door, there was a message that read, 'It is a sin to go barefoot. To cure this sin, come to Bonifacio, the shoemaker of the village.' The sandals that Bonifacio made had strong soles and were resistant to the relentless local weather, allowing the villagers to run after the prey, in the muddy swamps and walk on the dry savannah. Bonifacio's business also prevailed because, not only did he trade with money, but sandals would also be exchanged with natural produce such as pig, chicken or milk. Once Sula began sporting a pair of the very same sandals that the villagers admired, the news spread. Outsiders and animals began to gather to see the famous Sula Cointer, he even met the prestigious male Rhino, who later called on his wife, explaining to her that a terrible development had occurred. The Rhino's wife wondered what could be so terrible when things still remained calm within the jungle, so, disinterested, she turned away from her husband. However, she continued to think what could be worrying her husband so much, perhaps humans coming to hunt the animals, or Sula Cointer passing away or destruction of the park. Yet her husband quashed all of these worries as he continued to tell her,

"Sula Cointer had begun to wear sandals." His wife stared at him in disbelief,

"Wake up, you are dreaming! There is no way he could fit his feet into human shoes!" To which her husband replied,

"But Sula Cointer can't exactly walk like the men do, even when he is wearing shirts, trousers and sandals. All the Chimpanzees seem to seek to imitate the human race, and this characteristic of copying others isn't just present in them, but also in man himself. The men imitate each other to achieve success. I believe it is ignorance which causes someone to imitate another, a lack of innovation within their own thoughts."

What the Rhino said was true. For example, among the natives, if a neighbour began to successfully sell groundnuts, then others would begin to sell groundnuts in the same way. However, Sula Cointer desired, at any price, to be alike the villagers but the unnatural upright posture made him feel nauseous.

He decided to ask a friend for advice and immediately thought of The Griot's friend, the Tortoise, whom he was told, was exceptionally intelligent. Once in his presence, Sula explained to him how he wished to walk upright like the humans without the curve in his back, which he had. The Tortoise was surprised to hear these complaints from the Chimpanzee, considering that he had a heavy shell on his back and had never complained. After thinking long and hard, the Tortoise declared that there was no rational way to rectify Sula's issue and that he should seek to use witchcraft. The wizards were masters of miracles, and with a recommendation from the wise Tortoise himself, Sula prepared himself to contact them.

The following day, Sula Cointer and his cousins went to see the village wizard. The wizard lived far from the dwellings of the village; it was a common practice for wizards to avoid cohabiting with others. One reason for this, amongst many others, was that those who visited the wizards didn't usually want to be witnessed doing so. If you were to ask the villagers if they had seen the wizard first hand, they would answer that they never had. However, if you were to ask the wizard who had come to see him, he would list almost everyone in the village, as well as those who had travelled from other towns. The truth was that in reality, everyone had consulted the wizard at some point in their lives, hoping that he could improve their lives with miracles.

Upon arrival at the wizard's lodge, Sula explained how he wished to walk upright, undeterred by his curved Chimpanzee spine. The wizard replied simply that Sula's dilemma was just a small problem; his withered face resembled a walnut, as it creased into a wry smile,

"My collaborators will solve this problem, one way or another, on one condition; you bring me a Rooster and your problem will be solved."

Sula and his cousins spent the day roaming around the village in search of any sellers who were offering Roosters. The issue that Sula and his cousins faced was that Rooster symbolised power within the village, and nobody seemed to want to sell their power. As the sun began to set, Sula and his cousins returned to the wizard and described the struggle surrounding his request. The wizard accepted their words and pondered upon them for a while before his thought turned towards his worst enemy: The Chief. He was sure that the Chief had a hen house.

The Chief had denied the wizard land in the past and he had been seeking vengeance ever since. The wizard told Sula and his cousins that if they stole the Chief's Rooster, their problem would be solved.

The wizard described to them that due to their bodies, they would be able to climb the Chief's fences and steal the Rooster.

Sula and his cousins took to the Chief's home under the cover of nightfall; however, despite the farmyard being clear, space was under the watchful eye of guards and watchdogs who patrolled the fence day and night.

Sula looked for a way in but couldn't find one, while his cousins were frozen by their fear of the Dogs. Inspired by the terror of being ripped to shreds by the watchdogs, one of Sula's cousins came up with an idea,

"I remember that the wizard has his own henhouse. If we go back there, we can steal his own Rooster, what do you think?" Sula and his other cousin were relieved to be presented with an alternative to being at the mercy of the hounds and so they snuck off into the night to get some rest before commencing their plan at dawn.

As dawn broke, the Chimpanzees had made their way to the wizard's domain.

They watched as one the wizard's assistant opened the courtyard gates and slinked in undetected. Headed straight to the henhouse, they spotted a fat, young Rooster, who sat away from the rest of the hens. They quickly killed him, bagged him and immediately went on to see the wizard. As Sula and his cousins presented the Rooster to the wizard, he grinned greedily and inquired to how they got him, to which Sula said the Chief's yard, of course. Suddenly, the wizard ordered his assistant that she bring him the head of the Rooster and his blood in a bowl. When she laid them on the table in front of him, he began to call on the bad spirits, hissing that the owner of the Rooster would lose his legs, which Sula Cointer would inherit. However, as he spoke, the wizard noticed that his legs had begun to shake, his assistant growled that he should be careful, yet the wizard snapped back at her, claiming that he had never failed even one of his incantations. But as the sensation in his limbs worsened, he requested she bring his enchanted mirror, which would allow him to see the victim. As he looked hard into it, his own face stared back at him. "Oh dear," he said, "I believe something has gone terribly wrong." As the wizard realised what was going on, Sula's posture began to straighten and his legs lengthened, while the wizard felt all the strength drain out of his own until he lost all the power from them. As soon as Sula saw that his wish had been granted, he and his cousins quickly fled the scene, not looking back.

Watching them, the wizard recognised the trap he had been caught in, but too late, the head of the Rooster had already been cut and the curse was in action.

Thus, from that moment, Sula Cointer walked just like a human, and the wizard lost his ability to walk altogether.

The tale of the Chimpanzee who stole the legs of a man spread like smoke in the surrounding villages. People were puzzled with how a man could have his own legs stolen and when they learned how, they were shocked at how an animal could, so successfully and cruelly, trick a human. Some said that it was a sign that the future did not solely belong to men, that the minds of animals were developing, and now they could plot and think like men. Meanwhile, the animals in Virunga Park started to hold a high amount of respect for the Chimpanzee, Sula Cointer, as his name went down in history. Sula was proud of himself. Now, he could walk just like the other humans; however, his long arms always appeared disproportionate in comparison with the other men and also accentuated the shortness of his legs. As Sula was walking one afternoon, he felt the hot sun beat into his brow. In Virunga Park, there were two seasons; the wet, and the dry season. This was most definitely the dry season. During this time, the trees lost their leaves, fruits became rare and many animals migrated to areas that were more favourable. The corner where the Chimpanzees dwelt, was quiet, as most of the Birds had flown north in search of food. The village was also quiet; most of the inhabitants had left to visit family, sell, produce or trade, as there was no farming to be done. This silence lingered over the animals and humans, until the rainy season rolled on during the month of September. The first day that rain fell signified a great festival; everyone rejoiced, everyone was cheerful. The rain signifies food, for both the men and the animals; additionally, it was the time when the jungle was heaving with Caterpillars. The Caterpillars were favoured by the natives for their nutrition and would be roasted and consumed during the festival month.

Nevertheless, Sula Cointer's new legs, posture and respect inspired him to look for a job. Sula's search for work provided much entertainment for many of the villagers, however, Sula was happy to work menial jobs, such as clearing gardens for a small pay. Eventually, after Sula began demonstrating his great work, the Chief of another village approached him with the job of clearing an old building out in order to accommodate some guests.

The building was an old house left by the old colonies, which the village used as a hotel for foreigners visiting the area. At this particular time, it was occupied by a couple of European researchers, who had come to observe how animals behaved in Virunga Park. The researchers were prepared for the lack of hygiene products or plumbing in these unadvanced villages and one had brought blue chemical tablets, which eliminated bad smells from within the toilets.

So, one day when Sula was making his usual rounds of cleaning the toilets in the hotel, he found out that when he flushed the toilet, the water appeared to be bright blue.

Sula jumped back, startled. He watched in amazement how the water changed colour from clear to bright blue. Quickly, he ran to the tap to see if the water was blue there too, however, when he turned it on, the water flowed out clear. Sula concluded to himself that something was very wrong and left work disgruntled, determined to consult his friends and resolve this enigma. On his way home, he became aggravated, the only way the water could be that blue would be because he had been somehow bewitched. Sula visited the Tortoise and he advised Sula that he was worrying too much, little did Sula know that he had already heard about the European scientists and their products. So, Sula continued to ask other animals whether they had an explanation, to which Betty explained that when she flew over the ocean, the water appeared blue.

Thus, the animals accepted that the two must be linked somehow. When the Griot overheard this conversation, he was surprised to learn that the water in the ocean was blue and questioned how on earth the water could have made its way all the way to the hotel's plumbing? For this reason, Sula was advised not to go to work until this puzzle was solved. The other Chimpanzees took advantage of the situation in order to scare Sula; suggesting that the vengeful wizard had brought this curse upon Sula.

Sula Cointer sat at home, depressed and engrossed in the thought of all the salary that he would be losing because of what could be the wizard's revenge. What could he do now? Fortunately, The Griot visited the Chief of the new village on Sula's behalf and told him of the whole series of events leading up to the blue water. The Chief was shocked at the news and called his associates in order to contact the owners of the hotel and find answers regarding the blue water. After being quickly escorted to the Chief's hut, the hosts explained the reason behind the blue water; that it was down to the European hygiene products. At this news, the Chief, Sula and all of the other animals were hugely relieved.

However, after witnessing the situation, the male Rhino advised Sula that human intelligence would always be more advanced than his own, therefore, when imitating men, Sula would always encounter problems and obstacles.

Sula continued his work, earning his own small amount of money. So, when the festival of the Caterpillars came around, Sula was able to purchase trousers, a waistcoat and a hat.

Wearing his new clothes, and with sandals on his feet, Sula was dressed beautifully for the celebration of the rainy season. At the beginning of the festival, the villagers and animals made their way to the village square and as they caught sight of Sula Cointer dressed so elaborately, the inhabitants watched him curiously. As the celebrations went on, Sula had eaten too many fruits and was about to quickly find a faraway bush to, as traditionally was done at this festival, relieve himself as there were no facilities on site. As Sula was briefly on his way back into the jungle, The Griot advised him not to be in sight as there were many guards and security men patrolling. As he sat, he suddenly heard Birds high above him. Quickly, Sula rose up to investigate when he realised, he had been spotted by two security guards.

"What are you doing over there?" called out one of the guards. Sula's mind rushed, if he told them the truth, then he would find himself in trouble with the Chief. However, as the guards approached, Sula realised that there was no way to pretend that he wasn't doing what he was doing, as beside him, sat the evidence! In a rush of panic, Sula covered the evidence with his hat and attempted to look nonchalant as the guards came closer and closer. As the guard stood next to Sula, he demanded to know what was underneath the hat, to which Sula explained that he was tired of eating bananas and had come out to the bush to catch a few Birds for a barbeque later on, he went on further to describe that a couple of Birds lay underneath his hat.

However, this idea of an animal setting up a barbecue angered the guard, who replied, "Sir, you are not entitled to have a barbecue and I demand that you release those Birds immediately."

Sula Cointer, with no hesitation, and without collecting his hat, bolted the scene. Seeing the hat on the floor, the guard smiled and looked around to make sure he wasn't being observed and hummed to himself, "I, however, am entitled to have a nice little barbecue tonight!"

The guard crouched down, again looking around for witnesses, before lifting the hat to catch the Birds underneath. As he lifted the hat, he quickly grabbed at the floor with his hands, feeling something soft, he pulled back fast.

Gradually, a foul stench rose and his gut fell through his boots.

His initial instinct was to bolt to the river to wash, but what had happened to him since that moment, could never be reversed, forever more would he be made fun of and would be pointed at by the natives.

The Griot and some of his animal friends were strolling towards the jungle when Sula Cointer flew past them in a blur, shouting, "Danger!"

When the others tried to stop him and ask him what was happening, he refused to be slowed and so the others also began to run. When they all had arrived well within the confines of Virunga Park and away from the village, Sula explained to them what had just occurred with the security guard.

The animals stared in shock at Sula before deciding to stay hidden within the park, waiting in fear for the consequences to develop. However, that night was still, with no news.

The following day, The Griot walked to the village, bringing the story to the Chief and requesting that he protect Sula from any bitter revenge that the guard may wish to bring upon Sula. Yet, when The Griot finished explaining what had happened, the Chief was astonished, he realised that he was the same animal which had formerly caused harm to the witchdoctor. Despite this, the elders whom the Chief consulted on this issue suggested that it was, in fact, the guard's own greed which caused this feud, and that the guard deserved whatever consequence he experienced as a lesson for him to control his greed.

The news became quickly known in every household and soon after, the guard mysteriously disappeared for a week. Once he emerged from his hiding, he denied everything. The guard's close friend was outraged at the humiliation that his friend had undergone and took himself off to Virunga Park to find Sula and his cousins, after hours and hours of searching empty bush, he stumbled upon the corner of the jungle where the Chimpanzees thrived. As his eyes rose up, he saw two young Chimpanzees hanging off the branches. Immediately, he began hurling insults at the Monkeys who simply smiled back at him, once he had finished with his assault, they replied,

"Look at the way you walk, your legs would be so useful."

"I would do anything for those very legs!" The Monkeys approached the man menacingly, who, after seeing the malice in their eyes and the sharpness of their teeth, ran swiftly away back to where he came from.

As the man arrived back in the village, he looked white with fear and sweat. When the other men asked him what had happened to him in the jungle, he told them that he had seen a Leopard, who had attacked him.

As he sat at home, he began to ponder on the events, realising that humans were beginning to fear the Monkeys for their genius. Upon this knowledge, he concluded that they must have come from the same father.

Chapter 5

Turbulent Life of Insects

The major issues between man and the insects began with the Fly. A very long time ago, the Fly lived peacefully with men, sharing his life with the humans quietly. The Flies worked as a network, sharing information between one another. Thus, all the Flies knew what occurred, even far away from their dwellings, due to this chain of knowledge. On the other hand, the men only had the drum to transmit news in the evening when nature became quieter.

When the Birds rested and the night was still, the men would beat the village drums to communicate with nearby villages, but this method was inferior in comparison to that of the Flies.

Within one of the villages, a father and son had heard that there was work in a plantation, far from their humble home. Both the father and son were desperate for the money in order to feed the family, however, they had no idea of the route they needed to take to reach said plantation. Yet a Fly, whose sense of smell was inherently brilliant, knew exactly where to find the plantation and decided that he would help this father and son in their journey.

The father, son and Fly, all took to the road as the sun rose, walking along a long path, which took them to a railroad that they had to cross. The villagers and animals had not yet seen a railroad, but this one had been built to transport goods from the jungle to the city. They arrived very close to the railroad and heard a fast approaching whistle, which quickly turned into a bellowing howl, the Fly yelled that the group stop and wait for the train to rush past. The father and son stood in awe; they had never seen such a huge machine in their lives. Although, the son was taken back to a memory of when a car arrived at the village from the city, unable to move due to a punctured tyre. The villagers watched as the driver and passenger bent over the huge black wheel, considered how they pumped air into the rubber. The memory was clear in his mind, as these things seldom happened in villages like his.

The son, with curious eyes, followed the fast-moving wheels of the train as it passed, before asking his father, "Father, do they have to pump up the wheels of a train the way they did to the vehicle?"

The father, who was also unaware of this kind of technology, replied that the lives of those in the city were unexplainable. The Fly followed the conversation attentively, he had seen trains before and knew that the wheels were made of iron and there was absolutely no way of 'pumping them up'.

He had visited this area before the railway had even been constructed, he had protested against it and seen trains rush by ever since. Despite all this knowledge, the Fly made no comment but was astonished at the ignorance of the men. After many long hot days and nights, the Fly left the father and son at the plantation where they found the work they had so long searched for. They were to remain there for a few months, yet in that time, the Fly returned to the area around the village to spread the news about the ignorance of man. The Fly saw the father and son as morons and from this experience, believed that Flies were far superior in their intelligence. The news did not please the other villagers.

Three months passed and the father and son both returned home with sufficient money. Joyfully, they bought sugar, salt and various products from the market. However, this joy was short lived as they soon heard the tale that the Fly had told about them. This was how the animosity between the two species started. The villagers grouped together and decided to banish the Flies from the village, wishing never to see them outside of the jungle. It became a custom that the villagers would kill any Flies seen on their property without hesitation. However, as we witnessed, the Flies were not stupid. The Flies sought to find solutions to this frenzied human domination and violence, finding friendship in the Caterpillars, which they came across within the jungle.

The Caterpillars and Flies formed a close relationship, with the Caterpillars confiding in them about the difficulty that their slow mobility caused. The Caterpillars showed them the joys of sweet leaves and tasty bark, while, on the other hand, discussed the fear of being killed and eaten by the villagers. As the friendship developed, the Flies would fly everywhere to find sweet leaves and bring them to share amongst the Caterpillars. For this reason, the Flies felt in a position of great power within this relationship due to the dependence that the Caterpillars developed on them.

This was until one morning, after weeks of living side by side, the Flies noted that the Caterpillars had also somehow developed wings... The Flies were astonished at the way in which their humble, slow friends had become beautiful, strong creatures overnight! The Flies, now jealous of their colourful wings, demanded that their friends share their secrets.

In response to this demand, the Butterflies tried to convince the Flies that their body simply changes as they grow, however, the Flies did not buy this idea and immediately went to talk to other insects who lived in the same part of the jungle in the search for information. Our old friend, the Fly, went to consult an ant. The ant chuckled at the situation and advised the Fly that they should conduct an experiment, "What you need to do is find a beautiful Fly and couple her up with a male Butterfly. Then, we can see whether the child is born with wings or as a Caterpillar."

The ant gave a wry smile at his idea and the Fly quickly accepted the challenge and got to work. He found a gorgeous Fly by the name of Snuffs and presented her to his faithful Butterfly friend, who pulled the Fly aside before shouting at him, "This is abominable! We are not the same species!"

Yet, the Fly kept insisting, to the Butterfly's confusion. The Fly worked for weeks to ensure both the Butterfly's and Snuff's happiness, hoping and ensuring the two developed some kind of relationship. He would travel for miles to deliver delicious meals for the two to share and speak very highly of both in each other's presence.

One day, Snuffs finally got pregnant and produced eggs. The Fly watched over those eggs day and night, determined to find out the answer to his long-standing question. Unfortunately, as the eggs hatched, he observed that all the children had wings and all looked like purebred Flies. He did not hesitate to suspect that some sort of trickery was at work here. He was furious that, after all of his hard work and nourishment, another male Fly had intercepted his project.

The Fly despised the way in which Snuff and the Butterflies had betrayed him, despised the denseness and closeness of the jungle, despised the lack of sunlight and now looked longingly back at the village, believing it was now time for him to return.

When walking alone and pondering on his relationships with both men and the Caterpillars, the Fly met with a mosquito. They sat together and the Fly discussed with him all that had happened with him, the humans, the Caterpillars and Snuff. The mosquito listened with empathetic ears and, in exchange, he offered up the story of how the humans made fun of the 'mosquitoes and consequently how the mosquitoes began consuming their blood as vengeance. He explained how, as a result, man now fears the mosquitoes. He went on to describe how the power merits a strange kind of respect from the humans,

"Although, my friend, we mosquitoes aren't the only ones who can make the man fear us. A long time ago, the Flies brought a painful disease to the villages. Unfortunately, I can't go so far as drawing out a strategy for what you desire."

The mosquito advised the Fly, who stared intently at his new friend. The Fly reported back to the other Flies with all his new information; the older Flies explained the secrets of the illness while the younger ones ranted and raged about how the Caterpillars were traitors, that the humans loved them and thus they too had become the enemy.

The mosquito recommended that the Flies launch an attack on the humans, explaining that they needed to find a weakness that they could take advantage of, "For me, I have found it easy to attack the villagers at night during their slumber to suck their blood. The next morning, after my poison is in their bodies, they fall sick." He smiled. However, the Fly replied that he had no knowledge of how to inject poison into a man. To which the mosquito described the intricate way the human's skin was made up of tiny holes called pores, which serve as an opening to their body and a weakness for the man.

Thus, over the next weeks, the villagers were unknowingly plagued by Flies at night, who filled their bodies with disease while they slept. The villagers became ill in great numbers and the Flies increased their activity upon seeing this success. They began ambushing people while their minds were occupied with other things, most of these victims consisted of women working in the fields or men while they were hunting. For example, our old friend Bertrand, who hunted in the hot afternoons, concentrated with his gun on a Monkey and just at the very moment he intended to pull the trigger, he felt a sharp painful bite on his arm and misfired. This spreading of illness became an epidemic within the village. One day, Betty paid the Chief a visit, however, the Chief was trapped in an intense sleep due to a disease he contracted from a Fly bite. For the villagers, there was no escape; during the night, they were ravaged by mosquitoes and by day, they were targeted by Flies. It was for this reason that many of the villagers fled from their lives in the bush and moved to the city. Not only were the Flies biting now, but they were collecting diseases from the waste and cesspits and spreading it around the humans' homes too. The men decided to fight back.

The men and women discussed possible ways to regain the power but the solution came from a simple townsman who suggested straightforward cleanliness and hygiene. He described how hunters bring the germs from the jungle and raw meats to others, how travellers bring outside diseases into the village.

However, hygiene and cleanliness were difficult for rural villagers to implement, considering they only had very basic amenities and lived within a thriving jungle. The only hygiene that the natives excelled at, was dental care, even compared to the townsmen who used modern pastes and tools to clean their teeth. The villagers used tree roots and pastes to clean their teeth and from birth until retirement, they never suffered serious dental issues. The natives criticised the townsmen for their soft-stained teeth, which lost their strength and colour due to their sugary foods and excessive consumption of coffees and teas. In contrast, the natives' teeth were like ivory stones.

However, despite their brilliant dental hygiene, the villagers could not find a cure for diseases, such as malaria, caused by the mosquito and Fly attacks. They needed the help from the townsmen. Thus began the feud between the humans and the Flies…

Chapter 6
Rocambole, the Famous Boy

The history that we would read in this chapter, is the story of a young boy named Rocambole. It was the first name that his father had given him. His father was the famous Mr Bonifacio, who caught the disease of the Rooster, and he had a big belly, inflated like a pregnant woman. Mr Bonifacio, after being cured from his sickness, returned to his native village. But he was always annoyed by the children who made fun of him when he was walking on the street. Bonifacio received a bicycle, as a gift from the pastor, who treated him when he was sick.

Then at the village, he started a new life by roasting meat and making skewers to sell in the market. But when he passed with his bicycle on his way to the market, children followed him and shouted, "It's Mr Rooster," and he was very annoyed and insulted the children,

"I roosted your mother, go to hell." The children found this game very amusing and every day, they gathered in the street waiting for Bonifacio, on his way back. It became very annoying to Bonifacio and he decided to leave the village to, the peripheral of a big city, far away from the village, where he was unrecognisable by people and forgot the shout of 'Mr Rooster'. Most of the people in the big city had a TV screen and sometimes, electricity. Now, life for Bonifacio was a little bit different; not like in the village, where, as the darkness fell, people gathered around a fire. Bonifacio had money which he had saved. He purchased a small TV in black and white to spend his evenings before going to sleep, like every townsman. Every evening, when he turned on his television, there was a documentary film on. And the series was called *Rocambole,* which was the name of the protagonist of the film. Rocambole was a robber and swindler who had made a fortune from his dirty business. The gangster Rocambole always succeeded in his illicit manoeuvres. Bonifacio found this series very amusing and he became a fanatic of the series. Each evening, he remained in front of his small screen to follow the film, with his peanuts and cooked cassava. It was the new life of Bonifacio and he became a respected man without problems. He always earned money by selling his skewers.

A man, in life, should not be single, so Bonifacio found a woman to share his life with. In the following months, the woman became pregnant and later gave birth to a baby boy, and Bonifacio named the child, if you can imagine? The child was given the name 'Rocambole'. It was the belief of the natives that the name which is given to the child, produces the qualities of his predecessor, especially when the child is a teenager. And so, they avoided giving the child names such as misery, because the name would bring misery to the life of the child. They preferred rather, a name such as 'Blessing', considering that the child would be blessed in this life. Sometimes, they preferred to give names of animals, like 'Lion' or 'Leopard', thinking that the child would be a vigilant warrior like these animals. It was, thus, when one of the natives gave his child the name 'Fish' that the entire village made fun of him. He called his son 'small fish' and when he got older, he started calling him 'great fish'. Then the young man, 'Mr Fish', left the village, and never again went back to the village. Others came to visit their relatives, at least during the festivals. When the parents of Mr Fish complained about the behaviour of their son, people made fun of them by saying that fish always followed the current of the water, as a woman followed a rich man and, in both cases, it was very rare that this behaviour could be reversed. The idea of never going back settled on the ears of Mr Fish. He confirmed that the darkness of the village frightens him, especially during the night, when he wants to use the toilets. Because of this assertion, Mr Fish was right not to return to the village. But nobody in the village believed him. Thus, fish could never go in reverse because water entered his fins.

Rocambole, being a little boy, made too many whims, like a small child. But that did not disturb the parents. Young Rocambole always stole the toys of his friends and when he was hungry, he helped himself to the food by opening the pot without his mother's permission. On all these whims, the parents punished him, but they found the situation normal because Rocambole was still a kid. But at the age of twelve, the phenomenon appeared on Rocambole. Like the children of his age, he had to wear shoes to school. But young Rocambole, as soon as he got hungry, removed his shoes and sold them to the shoemaker in the market. The parents did not understand anything and in the evening, when returning home, the child came home barefoot. By selling his shoes, Rocambole invited his friends to share the food in a quiet place, out of view of other people. Rocambole liked to share food with his friends and that's why most of them thought of Rocambole as a true and perfect friend. Because some of them could not satisfy their hunger in their homes. Considering the child Rocambole, who liked to lose his shoes all the time, the neighbours ended up calling him 'the child without shoes'. They said that this child had a problem with shoes. One of them suggested that the father of Rocambole should check the toes of his kid well, because he must have chewed them and when fitting the shoe, it hurt him. But the parents checked well and the child had not chewed them and they had to buy other shoes because he had to wear shoes in school. Considering the pressure from the school to wear shoes, Rocambole started to have tantrums. He didn't like school because there was too much pressure for him; to wear shoes, to study, do homework, remain seated all day. All these things did not please Rocambole. Rocambole wanted freedom. The parents ended up being tired by the constant refusal of their son, who did not want to go to school. The child, Rocambole, preferred to trail around the town with his friends and sometimes to steal or to do small jobs, to get money. Rocambole wanted to carry out life like a street child and wanted to be free. He had the eye of a raptor, like the Bird flies in the sky, looking for a prey, Rocambole walked around the town, looking for money.

One day, an uncle came from the village to visit Rocambole's family.

As all the villagers did, he had brought some bags of cassava and maize to sell in the town. And on his way back, the money he had earned would enable him to buy necessities before returning to the village. After one month of transactions, the uncle finished and made a good profit on all the goods he sold.

One evening, after an intense day, Rocambole returned home empty-handed and very hungry. He found his uncle counting bank notes and the receipts of his goods. Rocambole was attracted by the movements of his uncle whilst counting the money. Rocambole went to sit in the corner of the living room, contemplating what his uncle was doing. The raptor was thinking of how to seize the bank notes. Rocambole thought of all the ways in which he could steal his uncle's money but had no success. The uncle had his money with him even while sleeping. He placed his wallet under his pillow. And during the night, whenever he went to the toilet, he took his wallet with him. Rocambole was following all the movements of his uncle.

During the day, when he went out, he put his wallet under his socks, and not in his pocket, and then he put on his shoes. The uncle was very careful, as though anticipating something evil would happen. In any event, the practice of all the villagers to be wary about the townsmen was a common habit. This was because they were easily targeted by gangsters, thieves, conmen etc. who trail around the town and marketplaces where people gather for shopping.

One day, Rocambole told his friends how his uncle had a pile of money because he was selling goods. He asked them if they had any idea how to take some banknotes from this person, because he was very vigilant, like an animal. They knew that the uncle travelled by the public bus. One of his friends, who was very astute, assembled a plan to thwart the uncle at the time when he would go up the bus. Rocambole had studied his movements during the day; all of his movements, like a true schemer. In the morning, the bus stop was packed with people who were going to work. People hustled themselves to get onto the bus. Rocambole preferred to remain out of the show. His four friends (whom we would call gangsters), followed the uncle very closely in the morning when he was waiting for the bus. Rocambole confirmed that his uncle always kept his wallet full of banknotes under his socks. At the moment when he was getting onto the bus, two gangsters moved fast and positioned themselves in front of Uncle and the other two remained closely behind him.

The uncle did not suspect anything, or that he was in the middle of four gangsters, and he was completely unaware of the plan they had. For Uncle, everyone came to take the bus during the rush hour and it was normal to have a scuffle. When the bus stopped, Uncle ran to go in and the gangsters also followed. The two gangsters who were in front got in first, followed by uncle.

But instead of moving forward, the two gangsters blocked the way, and the other two, who were behind, came to the side and pulled Uncle's shoes and socks and then his wallet. Uncle felt something on his leg and started to shout, but people were rushing to fill the bus. Nobody realised what had happened and the two gangsters who were behind, escaped with the wallet, giving up the socks and shoes that belonged to Uncle. Uncle was now in the bus and shouted, "Thief!"

People in the bus were surprised to see uncle barefoot and that he was shouting, "Thief in the bus." The two other gangsters, who remained in the bus, remained calm and commented with the other passengers that there were too many robbers in this country and that people do not want to work. On the next stop, the two gangsters got off the bus and went to meet their colleagues and master, Rocambole.

You should have seen the face of uncle, who cried for his money. He collected his pair of socks, shoes and began to walk like an insane person. The mother of Rocambole, who remained at home, saw Uncle returning in a deplorable state and asked him, "What is going on here?" Uncle explained that some robbers stole all his money. As usual, all the neighbours gathered around Uncle to listen to the story. But Uncle wondered how these robbers knew that the money was hidden in his sock. Each one was giving his point of view; one said that thieves could smell the odour of money. Another said that they detected the place where money was hidden through magic, because they worked with witchcraft. Uncle was overwhelmed and devastated. However, it was the work of the famous boy, Rocambole, who revealed to his gangster friends the place where Uncle hid the money.

In the evening, whilst returning home, Rocambole bought a small bag of flour for his mum and dad, and gave his mum some money. The mum was very happy, she blessed her son, then started telling Rocambole about the mishap of the uncle. Rocambole presented all manner of regret to the uncle for what happened to him and advised him to choose a better mode of transport when he had money. However, the money which

Rocambole had brought to his mum, was his uncle's money, that he had stolen and shared with his friends. The world was very malicious, as one could say, "The happiness of some people makes the misfortune of others." The villagers and natives were always victims when they came to big cities; being unaware of the urban way of life, and were confronted with all difficulties. They faced difficulties moving into an urban area, and then they became the prey of dishonest people, who benefitted from exploiting them. He didn't stay long in Rocambole's house afterwards, as was still very frightened by the situation that happened to him concerning the theft of his money. It was better to go back to the village instead of losing more goods, which he had already bought. On the other side, the raptor, Rocambole, was considered a good boy by his parents because he nourished the house. The principle of Rocambole was that despite all the goods, or the money he got, he never forgot his parents. He liked to buy food for his friends, to spend time with them, but at the end, he took the money and food to his parents too. Because of the fact that Rocambole participated in domestic expenditure of the family, the idea of attending school was completely given up.

Now the question was that, would a young boy like Rocambole be able to carry on his life correctly? Without education or instruction, the young man preferred to go seek a job somewhere else. In this life, to steal all the time was very risky.

Considering poverty, people also became very vigilant. Another day, Rocambole saw how one of his friends was thrashed by people when caught stealing in the market. Then, after that tie, many young people started to travel to the mining area to dig, instead of staying in the town doing nothing. The ones who arrived and found ores like diamond or gold, had their lives changed completely and they became rich after staying in the mining area. Rocambole, with the eye of the raptor, saw some of these people getting rich after staying in the mining area. When the life of Rocambole became very hard, he decided to try his luck, as 'who risks nothing, has nothing'. Life in the mining area was not easy. In the mining area most of the people slept in the open because there were no houses. People backed off, scattered everywhere, each in their own corner with their hut, to spend the night in, and protect themselves from the rain.

There was no sanitary place, and if need be, you would have to go and hide in a corner and relieve. Especially in this environment, one should not fall sick, because there were no doctors. Whereas mosquitoes were busy doing their business. If you asked the opinion of the mosquitoes who lived there, they would tell you that they were happy and that life was beautiful. Many young people had lost their lives only because of the aim of finding diamonds. Life was very hard in this mining area; it was full of people who came and sought fortune. It was the same with Rocambole, the raptor, he came to try his chance. The young girls in the big city made fun of young people when they were miserable and asked them to go and try their chances in the mining area. Because life in the big city became very difficult, especially for young people like Rocambole, who did not study and had no education, without work, the only possibility was to go to the mining area and have a chance.

Rocambole couldn't support his life in the bush. But to return empty-handed and start the life again with his parents was impossible. The raptor did not even sleep well. He thought he could steal something and disappear. But in this environment, everyone was vigilant, because Rocambole was not the only one to think of this. If somebody managed to find a precious stone, he did not say anything, even to the people surrounding him, for fear of being robbed. They dug deep holes, looking for precious stones. There was one in a thousand chance to find a precious stone and this was how they passed their time. In the evening, whilst returning, there was no good food, like Rocambole would get from his mum, it was necessary to disentangle from the rest to have food. Rocambole wondered to himself why he was born because life was becoming increasingly difficult. Some of them started to pray to God if He could help them find a precious stone. Rocambole looked at them requesting from God and questioned which world he actually was in; because he had never prayed in his life. Rocambole wondered whether God actually answered the priests. There were talks in the area that an old wizard, who lived far, was making incantations to people, who consulted with him and he was helping them find precious stones. One would know only the following day, when the person disappeared without informing anyone. It was only after one or two days that people would realise the disappearance. And it was normal for a person to disappear because that environment was not good. Everyone was jealous, and there was a risk to be killed if people found out that you had a precious stone. Rocambole was sharing life with an old man, who was there before him. The old man started to be very frank with him. He explained to him how life was in the area and that not everyone had the same luck. Some people could spend the whole year without finding anything. He promised to reveal a secret to Rocambole. The secret was that his companion of misery had decided to go and see the old wizard, because it had now been a year and he was still in the same situation. Rocambole tried to convince him not to go see the wizard, but he explained to Rocambole that a year had passed since he had left his wife and children in the city. He was afraid that his wife would find another man. Then he revealed to Rocambole that he had a precious stone and asked him if he could keep it until he came back. On his return, he was sure that he would have found another one after the consultation the wizard. The following day, the old man decided to leave the place and go to see the witch. The walk could take one day before arriving at the witch's place. He advised Rocambole to keep the stone well, and to expect his return, upon which they would share the nest egg together. That night, Rocambole did not close his eyes. He thought about the stone left by his friend. But the next morning, instead of going to the mining area, like any raptor, he changed his mind and decided to leave the place with the precious stone.

On his return to his parents, Rocambole had become unrecognisable due to the hard life of the mining area, and he was sick. In the evening, he presented the precious stone to his parents, and when they saw the stone, the parents were very happy and proud of their son. The following day, news spread around the area that Rocambole was back with a precious stone. One of the neighbours heard the news and was interested to purchase the precious stone. The woman had a plan in her head and explained it to her husband: she proposed to sell their compound and with the money, they could buy a diamond. But first, they needed to check the value of the stone. By selling the precious stone, they would be able to buy another compound much bigger than the first. The husband was not convinced. He advised his wife to be wary of this kind of transaction.

Rocambole's family were tenants and they wanted to sell the stone, especially to buy a compound.

The James couple asked the Rocambole family to allow them to initially check the authenticity of the precious stone and its value, as they had agreed to buy the stone. Rocambole's family gave them the stone for checking. The James couple went to contact a Pakistani man who was a specialist of precious stones, who confirmed that it was an authentic stone, which was worth $60,000.

Upon hearing that, the heart of the woman was filled with joy. By buying the stone for $20,000 from Rocambole family, they could resell it for $60,000 to the Pakistani man. However, the husband was reluctant because they had previously purchased the compound by making many sacrifices and by making rebate. Rebate was the system which went very well for people who had low income. That meant a group of people agreed to subscribe an amount of money and gave it to one of the participants. If they were, for example, a group of ten people, at the end of the month, one participant would receive the contribution of all those ten people. So, by the tenth month, everybody would have received the necessary amount. Thus, this was how they managed to buy the compound; the husband had participated in the rebate with his work colleagues. The woman, also being a saleswoman, had done the rebate with her friends. The money received from both sides allowed the James couple to buy the compound.

All the deals were carried out honestly and with confidence. The James couple sold their compound for $30,000 and brought the precious stone for $20,000.

They moved to live for a few days at their sister-in-law's place, whilst waiting to sell the precious stone. They explained to the sister-in-law that they were there for a few days, as they needed time to sell the precious stone. The hospitality custom obliged the sister-in-law to agree to accommodate them for a certain amount of time. On the other side, Rocambole's family had already planned their departure. Having received $20,000, Rocambole's family moved out to the countryside, where the compounds were less expensive. The news of the purchase of the precious stone was propagated all around the area and people watched as the poor Rocambole family moved.

All the neighbours knew what happened between Rocambole family and the James couple. Each one making their comments on the way. The fact that they were moving, was a success in that life. The area where Rocambole's family lived was very poor and everyone was jealous of the success of the person who left that place. Some appreciated the deal which they had made, but others were not happy because they knew that their life would soon change. At the time of the departure of Rocambole's family, some people were shouting in joy, wishing the family good luck. While other people were making fun of them, saying, "Here is the poor family which goes away elsewhere." In that area, people knew each other and the neighbours knew how Rocambole family suffered, but this also did not please others. The act of moving showed that people had a positive financial situation, and everybody knew the origin of their fortune. It was the precious stone brought by Rocambole.

After the deal with the Rocambole family, a friend suggested to the James couple to sell the precious stone to the Lebanese man, who he knew because he was a good purchaser. He reflected that as the Pakistani man proposed $60,000, it was certain the Lebanese man would give them more. The friend in question thought already about his commission because he took them to a potential buyer. The couple had brought their friend with them to the Lebanese man and presented him with the stone. The Lebanese man checked the stone with a magnifying glass and declared that the stone was fake. The three people, feeling demoralised, decided to go back and see the Pakistani man, who had told them that the stone was good and gave them an evaluation.

Upon arriving to the Pakistani man, he took the stone and went to check, but after two minutes, he came back, saying that they must be joking with him.

Mr James asked him, "What do you mean we are joking with you?"

The Pakistani man said that the stone was not the one they had brought to him the last time; this one was a fake. Mr James collapsed at that time. The Pakistani man and some people brought water and threw it onto Mr James to wake him up!

Mr James, his wife and their friend did not understand what had happened to them. James looked at his wife in a bad mood and said, "The mother of my children, what have you done to me, have you changed the stone?" Because she was the one that was keeping the stone since they bought it from Rocambole family. James addressed the word to his wife by calling her the mother of his children to remind her that he was the father and the husband and it was not the time to play any dirty tricks. It was necessary to look at the tie which linked them. Mrs James looked at her husband, swearing that she had not done anything wrong and had not changed the stone. The Pakistani man told them that this stone was fake and different to the first one. But where was the first stone?

It was a question without answer, because no one could answer it. They came back home crying. For the moment, they were being accommodated by their sister in-law, after having sold their compound. What explanation would they give to the people? James was still thinking how a true stone could transform into a bad one.

It was a mysterious thing that had happened. Back home, everybody was sad about the news and some neighbours came to console them. Then an old woman, a mother of one of the neighbours, advised them that in life it was necessary to be discreet. These kinds of things should not be revealed to anyone, because you don't know the state of their soul. Not everybody would be happy for the success of your soul and wizards would always take advantage on good occasions like yours and act. It was for sure a wizard amongst the people had heard the news and transformed the stone into a fake one. She told them the story of her nephew who wanted to travel to Europe. By having a visa in his passport, he praised himself everywhere and told people he would be travelling to Europe. The day of his travel, he arrived at the airport and when he presented his passport, the photograph was not of him but of an old man he didn't even know. The immigration officer stopped him because the photograph was not of him. The nephew missed his travel and could never travel again to Europe.

Thus, it was always necessary to be careful and discreet in this life especially when you were engaged in business like that. You made your transactions by exposing it to everyone, not knowing there was a wizard in your environment. In the future, you should be wary about people, and do not have confidence in people, especially when it is about business. That was a lesson.

Not everyone was nice and not everyone appreciated the success of others. Here was how James and his wife became the unhappy ones, when Rocambole and his family disappeared in nature.

Chapter 7

The Hyena: Animal Parasite

The Hyena, as we know, was a parasitic animal, which lived at the expense of others. Their nasty reputation made it no surprise that they had become renowned to hiss and spit at passers-by. Their animosity towards others and their parasitic nature came from the fact that they couldn't run as fast as other predators to catch their own prey, thus they survived by hijacking the prey of others.

The jungle was very favourable for herbivorous animals who could easily find sustenance within the dense vegetation. However, carnivorous animals were required to prey upon these herbivores. This created issues for the carnivores, as hunting was not easy, especially chasing after swift Antelope or gazelles. The easiest animals for Hyenas to catch were the bush rats, which emerged at night to forage for food. Although these rats were far bigger than domestic rats, an adult Hyena would need three or four of them just to feel satisfied.

So, the story we will follow focuses on our small Hyena friend, Pakoso, who accompanied Betty to see the King Lion. That small Hyena had now grown, the wise and loyal soul who refused the offer of the Lion's soldiers now had to scavenge like the others to survive. When Hyenas were on the prowl, they resembled a criminal gang and anyone that crossed them, who was weaker, became regarded as prey. Pakoso and his gang had become sick and tired of nourishing themselves solely on rats. One told the news of the Lion Chief who would throw a huge festival in honour of his daughter's marriage. The hunters would hunt an enormous number of cows and Goats in the run up to this festival. This was when Pakoso's gang decided that they would find where all the meats were kept for storage…

In the neighbourhoods within and around Virunga Park, there were different tribes, which were scattered across the lands. Each tribe had its own totem and own beliefs. The Lion tribe wore masks, which mimicked the face of Lions and their totem was engraved with stories and images of Lions. The Lion tribe aimed to be strong and valiant as those were properties seen in the Lions. If a thief was to steal from the Lion tribe, the tribe would call upon their ancestors and fate the thief to be ravaged by Lions, or to forever be cursed with nightmares of Lions. For this reason, others avoided having problems with this particular tribe.

The Lion Chief had killed many cows, Goats and sheep for the festival. In the traditional way, he had roasted and salted the meats in order to keep them for a long time. After this preparation was done, the meats were stored in a secret place, hung on racks and covered in sheets and leaves from the trees.

The Chief recruited many watchdogs and lookouts to guard the meats and supervise the area. The news of this great store of meat had spread far among the natives and animals before reaching the Hyenas. In any case, the Lion Chief really couldn't imagine anybody risking bewitchment and revenge in order to steal from them, it had never happened in their history. However, the Hyenas continued to plot to take out the watchdogs and have clear access to the meat.

They watched and waited for a stormy night when the rain would drown out the sound of the Dogs and so the surrounding people would not awaken. The Hyenas were fearless, especially when food was at stake.

The night came and the rain pounded loud on the dry ground, the Hyenas launched their attack on the watchdogs and scattered them, seizing all the meats before scampering off back into the night. Before the festival started, the Hyenas had eaten all the meats and were no longer hungry. However, one older Hyena still desired to have more and returned back on his own to the Lion tribe's territory. However, this time the old Hyena was killed on site and his presence convinced the tribe that Hyenas were behind the theft of their meats.

Even the Dogs confirmed to the Chief, who had previously assumed the Dogs had monopolised against him, that it was, in fact, the Hyenas who had attacked them. This discovery led to a mass hunting of Hyenas by the Lion tribe. The Hyenas lived in fear, trekking far to avoid the Lion territory. Pakoso decided to take refuge with his old friend, The Griot. When he arrived, the Tortoise was also there, he explained to them what had happened with his companions and what they did to the Lion tribe, and The Griot listened with a stern face. He was afraid to keep Pakoso in case he was discovered, then there would be awful consequences for the both of them; therefore, The Griot decided to send Pakoso to his friend, who lived in the city park, away from Virunga Park and the danger that it brought to Pakoso. Later that night, the Tortoise called upon his ancestors to protect his good friend Pakoso, advising him to pray often as his days may be limited. He explained to Pakoso that the rumours about the witchcraft and curses from Lion tribes were true, that he would begin to dream of Lions at night, hallucinate about Lions and live in fear until he reaches an early death. Pakoso began to panic, not knowing what to do. The Griot listened with a melancholy silence, as he knew that the words the Tortoise spoke were true, all the Hyenas would be kept awake by dreams of Lions until, one by one, they were devoured by them. The Griot arranged that his nephew would accompany Pakoso to his brother's home in the Great City, hoping that perhaps being far away from Virunga Park would mean that the harmful spirits would not reach him.

Pakoso graciously accepted The Griot's suggestion, then turned to the Tortoise, "Are there any remedies to fight the bad spirits of the Lion tribe?"

The Tortoise replied that there were remedies, which would call upon spirits to protect him; however, due to the fact that Pakoso had perpetrated the crime, he was not certain that the spirits would work in his favour. Therefore, his best option was to flee. So, that same night, The Griot brought Pakoso to his nephew, who would make the journey to the Great City with him. Before setting off, Pakoso asked The Griot if he would keep that night's plans a secret.

"You have my word," replied The Griot solemnly, before embracing Pakoso and watching him flee off into the night.

After walking for four days and nights, the two finally arrived at the big city. The Griot's nephew announced their arrival with great relief and elation before briefing Pakoso about the culture.

"Just be quiet and respectful of the city people and don't steal anything! The Griot's brother loves animals as much as The Griot himself, so he will take good care of you, as long as you behave..."

Pakoso listened with humble eyes and promised that he wouldn't disappoint anyone, remembering the kindness of The Griot and the Tortoise, who even mentioned that, in all his years, Pakoso may be the first intelligent Hyena he'd ever met!

***

It was the first time that Pakoso had ever been in a city, and he was taken aback by the herds and herds of people all travelling in different directions. The house of The Griot's brother was a little further out from the Great Urban Station and Pakoso was advised to mostly stay within the grounds of this home.

However, there was a square not too far from the house, where Pakoso would take in some fresh air from time to time. Pakoso remained calm and followed any advice given to him. However, one day Pakoso grew tired of remaining within the grounds and stepped out in the square. An advert caught his eye, it was a panel with a screen, rotating pictures and adverts. Pakoso stared at this panel in awe, he had seen some adverts before but none that moved like this. He sat and watched as every 30 seconds a new advert would replace the old one. First, he saw a woman posing with a skin cream and thought to himself whether they could create a product for his skin and how great that would be. He began thinking about what life would be like as an animal without the pungent and overpowering smell of the jungle on his fur.

However, to his great alarm, as the picture of the woman faded, an image of a roaring Lion appeared on the screen. Pakoso immediately stood up and turned away from the advertisement panel and attempted to steady his mind. He didn't want to see the image, but curiosity drove him to turn and glance at the panel again, only to see the same image of the woman again. He rubbed his eyes and remembered what the Tortoise had said to him, as his eyes readjusted, he, once more, saw the roaring Lion staring back at him. Running back home, he thought to himself that the Tortoise's prophecy was coming true, and soon death would strike him. The people witnessed him hurry home and how he cowered in the corner on his return. Pakoso curled into himself and remembered the words of warning he had received, how he would see Lions in his dreams and hallucinations, and how this was the beginning of the end. People asked him what had disturbed him so much. However, Pakoso lied and reassured them that he was simply feeling ill, unwilling to tell them of his criminal history and now his curse.

When The Griot's brother returned home, he found Pakoso trembling in his quarters. Immediately, The Griot's Brother went to his neighbour, who was a doctor, in order to get some medication for Pakoso. However, the doctor insisted on coming to see Pakoso himself. After viewing his condition, he concluded that he did indeed have a high fever, however, it was nothing that a minor medication couldn't cure. The neighbours often visited Pakoso and tried to find remedies of explanations to his condition, some said he had 'the countryman's disease'. This was a condition that some believed was brought about when those from the country come to the Great City, due to the change in environment.

However, Pakoso spent days wrapped in blankets, and every time he thought about the image of the Lion on the advertisement panel, his fever grew worse as fear took over his body. He was unable to sleep for the terror of dreaming of Lions and the medication didn't seem to give him any comfort.

It was for this reason that some say that ignorance kills and that simply the sheer belief of superstition was the only reason it affected a sufferer. People left their houses to watch how Pakoso's condition developed. Pakoso explained to the people that, every time he closed his eyes, he saw the Lion trying to devour him. To which the people would try to reassure him that there were no Lions in the city. As the people gathered around him in the small hours of the morning, they agreed that it was no longer a fever that he was suffering from, but a disease of the imagination. The city people were aware of how their indigenous cousins entrusted in spirits and superstitions too much and as a result their minds were negatively affected; therefore, while some neighbours thought that perhaps Pakoso was indeed being haunted by a bad spirit, other questioned the images he saw in his sleep; was it really a bad spirit? An older man suggested that it was a good idea to bring the Hyena to a healer, who could tell if he was really under threat and, if so, by who. The people of the city separated illness into either a bodily illness, or an illness of the mind. Doctors could cure bodily illnesses but illnesses of the mind could only be cured by healers.

For the moment, Pakoso was housed in a home guarded by Dogs, who were seen as animals able to ward off bad spirits and thus he was able to sleep quietly. During the night, if the Dogs sensed the presence of a bad spirit, they would begin to bark loudly in order to frighten it off. One of the Dogs reassured Pakoso that they call upon their ancestors to protect them from evil and that he would be safe under their watch.

The Dogs themselves had never seen a Hyena before and wondered where this large Dog with a small tail had come from. The young Dogs poked fun at Pakoso's tiny tail, large mouth and strange odour. The older Dog interrupted their jeering and explained that the Hyena was not a nice Dog, but a wild animal from the bush who ate rats and scavenged. Pakoso simply stared back at the Dogs with saddened and tired eyes. He hoped that one day he could advise his fellow Hyenas not to steal, helping them to avoid the nightmare, which he was currently experiencing.

He turned to the young Dogs and stated in a low voice,

"Never steal the foods of others, it may bring you much misfortune." After a moment, one of the Dogs suddenly replied,

"Are you a robber? Is that how you caught the disease?" To which Pakoso sat silently, wondering whether to tell them the truth. Finally, the Hyena decided to tell the Dogs the full story, as he believed that as he was about to die anyway, there would be no harm in revealing his secrets. Upon hearing what had happened; about the hallucinations, about the black magic of the Lion tribe and the curse, the old Dog explained that the disease would be very difficult to cure as the healers would ask a lot of money in return. He asked Pakoso what he was going to do as he could not rely on The Griot's brother as he wouldn't pay a penny for Pakoso's problems.

"Then I expect death," replied Pakoso. Saddened by the situation, the Dogs and the Hyena curled up to sleep.

A small puppy nudged his father and whispered, “How would we defend ourselves against a Lion? If he comes here looking for the Hyena, surely he would kill us all.”

“We can bark and warn off these bad spirits, other animals can fight, we can bark.”

***

The next day, the puppy asked his father whether he could play outside the plot; however, his father refused, explaining that anywhere outside of the plot was insecure and that he must stay with the pack at all costs, near Pakoso. However, when all of the Dogs dosed off for a nap, the puppy snuck out to find his friends through a gap in the fence behind the house and through an alley. He and his friends ran as children do and ended in the sight of Pakoso. The puppy wondered whether he would ever see visions like him. Childish curiosity pushed him to go and see the advertisement panel, which triggered the images.

He made his way to the square and sat in front of the panel, taking in the image of a woman and a beauty product, just as the Hyena had described.

However, the panel changed and displayed a picture of a strong Lion, which promoted the strength of a product. The puppy was surprised that it was this image that had frightened the Hyena so much. His friends grew bored and begged him to come away from the panel and play but the puppy focused on the image.

Intelligently, it occurred to the puppy that it wasn’t a vision of a Lion that Pakoso saw here, but simply the advert and due to his superstitions, he believed that he was hallucinating. On figuring this out, he ceased playing with his friends and ran straight home to announce the news.

In the evening, when everyone was present and gathered around the fire, the puppy stated that he had found the magic that would save Pakoso. His father and the other Dogs looked at one another, wondering who had taught this puppy to be so foolish. However, the puppy assured Pakoso that he would not die, and the next morning, he would give him the magic potion that would allow him to sleep well and have no hallucinations. Nobody had any idea what the puppy was talking about and all decided to go to sleep and see what would happen by morning.

Very early that morning, the Hyena rose and asked the puppy to give him the remedy. The puppy asked Pakoso to follow him, as he did so, the other Dogs stayed close behind. They arrived at the square and both sat in front of the advertising panel.

"Look hard at the panel," ordered the puppy.

Pakoso fixed his eyes on the panel, as well as all of the other Dogs. The image of the woman with the beauty product was displayed on the screen, laughing. Pakoso began to move, muttering that it was the same as last time. However, the puppy stopped his attempts to move and told him to keep watching. At that moment, everyone watched as the image changed to the Lion on the panel. Pakoso remained calm and felt incredibly stupid. Everyone realised that it was this image, which induced the fever due to Pakoso's belief in black magic.

On the way back home, Pakoso did not stop swearing in embarrassment, "Bloody Hell! I want to die like a chicken." He decided he no longer wanted to stay in the big city and wanted to return to the bush. The father of the puppy was filled with pride and congratulated his son for his intelligence and for saving the life of another animal. From that day, he boasted to others that he had a genius in the family. When they returned home, Pakoso threw away all of his painkillers and medication and swore he would never be an animal as stupid as a Crocodile ever again. In Virunga Park, the Crocodile was regarded as an idiot. This was because he fled from the rain and took refuge in the rivers. Thus, in effect, it fled water and found refuge in water.

So, to never be stupid again, Pakoso swore to never steal again. This stealing brought him terrible luck, but now he would return to the bush as a warrior.

The future belongs to both man and animal. Beings can always eat what nature gives to them but they should never consider each other as prey.

Chapter 8
Mister Rooster

The man who falls pregnant and carries a Rooster who shouts in his belly.

Animosity is a persistent ill feeling, which brings harm. Animosity appeared in a carnivorous or wild animal when he was hungry as another creature became prey; it also appeared when they had to defend their territory. For example, in the corner of the jungle where Monkeys and Chimpanzees thrived, they were hostile if there was a snake among their presence. This was because a snake was a poisonous animal, which bit and threatened every animal he came across. On seeing this predator, the Monkeys let off a stupefying cry to alert their accomplices of an intruder; this was also heard when the Leopard slinked into their territory. Among the animals, there were some who cohabited together, for instance, herbivores such as Zebras and Antelope. They lived together and share the grass which they ate. The same Monkeys accepted the presence of herbivores. However, they simply did not accept carnivores. Herbivores such as Elephants did not interrupt the Monkeys' peaceful lives as all they ate were large leaves, allowing the Monkeys to remain relaxed and go about their daily lives. On the other hand, the creatures that the Monkeys would not let intrude on their land included Lions, tigers, Leopards and Hyenas. Yet, there was one animal who could not be so easily categorised: this was man. Man had been known to be very aggressive and territorial, while also being known to have a very developed memory and the capacity to reason, which prevented signs of animosity to his peers.

The story that we will follow describes the situation between two neighbours living in the same village. They hated each other because one had possibilities while the other had none. Fulgence had possibilities because he was connected with his brothers and cousins who lived in town. His family often sent money and supplies such as cement bags in order to build. However, Uncle Bonifacio did not have anybody to help him and his house was built with earthenware terracotta with a roof of straw. Most of the houses in the village were built with terracotta or wood, so a house built with cement indicated that the inhabitant must have some prestige.

One day, Uncle Bonifacio had found a nest with a baby Owl in the bush, he took care of this baby Owl until he grew and was able to fly. Then, once able to fly on his own, he trained the Owl to fly over the space of his choice. Uncle Bonifacio, one day, noticed that his neighbour, Fulgence, had made a foundation all around his small terracotta house. Another day he found a bricklayer working in Fulgence's plot.

So, on next seeing his neighbour, Uncle Bonifacio questioned him about such developments. Fulgence replied with an air of arrogance that he was building the next house of brick and cement. The foundations were deep and ready, but it wasn't necessary to dive into the heart of Uncle Bonifacio to see how he suffered from jealousy. Every day, he would grit his teeth upon leaving his own house and feel nauseous at the sight of his neighbour's development. His neighbour was a native like himself but had the opportunity to upgrade in such a way.

The following day, Uncle Bonifacio went to the Chief to ask him whether a villager could build a house of cement because everybody else had houses made from the traditional terracotta and straw. However, the Chief replied that each person had the right to build their house in whatever way they chose, whether it was from terracotta or cement. We know that in big cities, the inhabitants had to apply for the right to build in certain ways, yet this knowledge did not sway the Chief's view upon the matter. On his return home, Bonifacio tried to convince his neighbour to lend him a couple of cement bags so that he also could begin to rebuild his house. However, this request was met with a firm refusal, as Fulgence explained his cement was a gift and thus could not be borrowed. Bonifacio had become insane and furious upon watching his neighbour create such architectural wonders. As the walls rose, they reinforced his own sorrow.

The Owl was an indigenous metaphor for misfortune. For the people, the Owl, as well as the cat, was an animal which cooperated with bad spirits. Thus, Bonifacio trained his Owl to terrify Fulgence in total secrecy. The Owl would perch upon Fulgence's wall and sing in the dead of night, this noise was as terrifying to the natives as the sound of the mountains crashing to the ground.

The villagers would fear the sinister way in which the Owl, unlike the other Birds who sing sweetly at the break of dawn, chose to announce the blackness of night. The people understood this Owl's song to foreshadow a terrible misfortune for Fulgence. Every night, while Fulgence and his family were tucked into bed, he would be awoken by the eerie sounds of the Owl. This lasted around a month before his wife decided to leave, unable to take the maddening and torturous torments of this Owl. On this day, Fulgence was forced by fear to visit the village wizard, who could communicate with the bad spirits and could cancel his misfortune. The wizard replied with a wry smile, immediately suggesting that it must just be his in-laws playing a nasty trick on him.

"That is why your wife has left with the children, then when whatever calamity occurs, they will be safe…" Fulgence accepted this and decided that his father-in-law must be attempting to illustrate Fulgence as evil due to a jealousy of his home.

When Bonifacio heard of this rumour, he simply laughed to himself at Fulgence's foolishness and continued his malicious games. On that day, he bought palm wine to celebrate his exploits and drank it until he was drunk. As he knew that the wizard was aware of the Owl, he decided to give the antics a break for four days. After the first few days, Fulgence believed that whatever curse was upon him had been lifted and began negotiating with his wife about her return with the kids. His in-laws, who were unaware of the wizard's allegations, advised her to resume living under her marital roof. Therefore, the family spent a happy week together again, undisturbed by the malevolent Owl.

The house at this point had very high cement walls, and the last step to be completed was to place the solid roof on top. To see Fulgence's house at such a finished state, made Bonifacio feel sick. Jealousy had corroded his heart and the following week he resumed his shenanigans with the Owl. Upon hearing the familiar and terrible sound of the Owl's cries that night, Fulgence faced a total dilemma. He could give up the house he had worked so hard to complete and move away, or he could remain on that plot and confront whatever terrible situation befell on him. Fulgence had no idea what the right choice was.

One evening, Fulgence had bought a pack of peanuts and was eating them on his way home from work. He felt good. He felt the same refreshing joy that one would feel when sipping ice-cold spring water on a searing hot summer's day.

For a second, Fulgence was able to momentarily forget his nightly struggle. It was raining, and puddles emerged within the dips and cracks in the ground. He stepped carefully, jumping every now and again to avoid wetting his feet. It was in this post-rain setting that Monkeys were also most joyful and they swung in the trees surrounding the village observing Fulgence. They contemplated his unhappiness, and also watched as he leapt between puddles. As Fulgence walked, a large package appeared to fall from the sky right in front of his feet, splashing a wet puddle across his face. The package of cow dung. Immediately the Monkeys began shouting and screeching that this cruelty was an abomination and that it was the Owl who had dropped this in his path before flying away.

The unhappy Fulgence stopped eating his peanuts, spun around and went to contact The Griot. Fulgence contemplated that if it was an Owl who had dropped this on him, then it surely had been sent by someone, but who? The Griot listened to his concerns and said that he would talk to the animals in order to find the culprit. As the Owl was a flying animal, he attempted to recruit Betty to spy on the airspace around Fulgence's property. However, Betty refused, stating that she was a woman of principle and was against spying on others.

Despite the Griot's attempts to persuade her, she stood firm. She was afraid that by spying on this Owl, she would be putting her own life in danger as the Owl had sharp claws while Betty had none. The Griot accepted Betty's point and then went on to the Monkeys and talked with Sula Cointer. The Griot asked him to locate where the Owl comes from and goes to hide, and to do so quietly and discreetly.

The Monkeys, after observing the Owl overnight, reported to Fulgence that at night, the Owl made his way from Bonifacio's home to Fulgence's house.

However, Fulgence brushed this knowledge off, not understanding what motive Bonifacio could possibly have to cause him trouble. Yet, as Fulgence reflected upon this a little while, glancing back to the recent conversations about his construction with the man, he concluded that this was a torment motivated by jealousy. Immediately, Fulgence was driven to seek out the wizard in order to inflict a vengeful wrath upon Bonifacio, as was custom within the village when one had been wronged. Nonetheless, he decided that he didn't want to contact the nearby wizard as he was the one who believed that the culprits were his in-laws. His cousin from town advised Fulgence to contact another wizard from a different region, who was renowned for his great power. His cousin described how this wizard was known by many to influence the outcomes of football matches in order for his team to win each time. This wizard seemed perfect. What was more, the wizard was far away and so whatever business they conducted would take place away from the curiosity of the other villagers.

Fulgence brought his Goat to the wizard and discussed with him that he should not kill Bonifacio, but simply make his life very difficult as a consequence of his terrible behaviour. Fulgence insisted that Bonifacio had to pay for all of the trauma he caused to his family with that Owl.

In response, the wizard wryly noted that he was an expert in stomach diseases, "Many women come to me to cast evil like this upon their rivals. Usually, I advise them to put a stone in the belly of the rival, rendering her unable to conceive…" the wizard pondered for a moment, eyes resting on Fulgence's resolute brow, "as Bonifacio is a male, let us put a Rooster in his belly that will sing each morning to announce the arrival of a new day and your liberty."

Thus, the wizard requested that Fulgence bring him a Rooster. He consulted him on the way in which he needed to kill the Rooster at 3 am as to ensure all passes in silence. Fulgence had to prepare the Rooster with a rich sauce and invite the scoundrel for a fine home cooked dinner.

Bonifacio was unaware of the scheme that was taking place. Poverty was an evil, which was difficult to avoid for these natives and so it had been a few days since Bonifacio had eaten particularly well. Bonifacio had been attempting to keep his hunger at bay with cassavas, Caterpillars and anything he stumbled across in the bush. So, when his neighbour invited him round for a meal cooked by his wife, adorned with peanuts and walnuts. However, as he walked into the aromatic home of Fulgence, it was the delicious scent of the juicy roast chicken that caught his attention. After being seated, fuelled by insatiable desire, Bonifacio did not finish his mouthful before shovelling more chicken in.

He spoke through gulps of the roast and once he was finished, he leant back in his chair, satisfied.

Many days passed and nothing seemed to happen to Bonifacio. However, after a month his belly began to grow. He suspected nothing malicious as men of a certain age in the village were expected to put on a few pounds. His belly did not stop there; it continued to inflate like a pregnant woman until it grew so big that Bonifacio found it difficult to walk. The people of the village were astounded by his sudden and dramatic stoutness; it had progressed far past the normal weight gain seen in older men.

One morning, to his unbearable surprise, Bonifacio awoke to the sharp cry,

"Coco Ricoo!" Waking to the sound of Roosters was normal in the village, as they did not have watches or alarm clocks and thus relied on the announcements of these Birds. However, what wasn't normal was that this particular ear-splitting cry came from Bonifacio's very own stomach. At first, he wanted to shout and cry for help, but he remained silent to make sure this wasn't just a strange hallucination and that the noise was coming from his stomach.

After days passed with Bonifacio lying immobilised in bed with the Rooster's loud crowing vibrating his body at each dawn, he became so distressed that his mind even wandered to thoughts of suicide. He didn't leave his plot and only had his Owl for company as well as a hunter friend who came to check up on Bonifacio each morning. One morning, he hadn't called. He would greet him, give him the news of the town and make sure he was alright. Impressed with the size of his belly, his friend had asked him,

"How are you feeling?" To which Bonifacio replied that he believed he had been cursed with an incurable disease. His friend attempted to boost his moral, consoling him that having a big belly was not an awful problem.

"It is not the size which is the problem, rather, the issue is that there is a Rooster inside of me. He crows every dawn." His friend jumped back at this curious announcement, struck with disbelief. How could there possibly be a live Rooster inside of a man? Once he was again able to form words, he solemnly noted,

"This is a very delicate situation. I think it's necessary to consult the healer in order to save your life, my friend." He swallowed before adding, "Where could such a curse have come from? Did you steal from someone? Have you killed anyone? Have you stolen another man's woman?" Bonifacio shook his head to all of these usual suggestions, and they agreed that he needed to see the Chief, and not remain alone in the house.

During their slow journey to the Chief's quarters, the news spread across the village, yet people greatly doubted that Bonifacio really had a Rooster in his belly. The only way to be convinced of his existence was to be within Bonifacio's presence at the break of dawn when his Rooster crowed from within. The Chief shared these same doubts and so permitted Bonifacio to stay in his home, and sure enough, the Chief awoke to the crowing of Bonifacio's stomach. The whole scenario was almost too incredible for the Chief to understand and he immediately agreed that Bonifacio should go to the healer. As the villagers heard that the rumours were true about Bonifacio, all were desperate to hear the Rooster for themselves and thus he was given the name, Mister Rooster.

Mister Rooster walked slowly, with his hands behind his back, supporting his strained spine, aching from the weight of the Rooster. His friend never gave up, helping him walk, eat and drink.

He remained determined to reach the healer and restore Bonifacio's health. He avoided the mockery of the villagers, which came from even the high nobles who joked about Bonifacio's ability to see his own manhood and surrounded his steps with sniggers and stares.

For Mister Rooster, he believed he was cursed as the healer refused to look after him. He had explained that this curse was far beyond anything he was powerful enough to cure. Furthermore, the village wizard refused to come into contact with Mister Rooster for fear that he would be infected by whatever bad spirits lay inside of him. Mister Rooster and his faithful friend searched and searched for help but could find no assistance…

Once a month, the priest celebrated mass in the village on the last Sunday of every month. Mister Rooster's friend suggested that he should contact the priest, perhaps he would have the answers. So, on that ultimate Sunday, as per usual, the Christians of the village dressed in their best wear for the Sunday mass. Mister Rooster also dressed, arrived at the church early and sat at the front of the assembly to ensure that the priest would see him well. As the people filtered in and caught sight of Mister Rooster, quiet grumbles could be heard assuming that he was seeking help from the priest. The villagers ridiculed him, jeering that he had caught a curse rather than an ailment, they wondered why he didn't just beg forgiveness from the man who caused him evil. Before entering the church, a villager had informed the priest that a patient was seeking his aid in the church, the priest was intrigued. Not many people attended his mass looking for medical assistance, the habit of those villagers was to go to the healers in these cases. When the priest arrived in the church, everyone was calm. The building itself was simply a hut, where the villagers sat on each side, leaving a passage between them where the priest now walked, glancing to each side of him, curious to locate the patient. All was quiet, and as he reached the front, he saw a man sitting with a huge belly protruding under his shirt. However, the priest saw this as normal and thus believed that the information given to him about a patient being in the crowd must have been false. He decided to start the mass. If a patient was there, then he would find him afterwards. Thus, mass was underway, the faithful sang, and absolutely nothing abnormal occurred. In the middle of mass, when all were focused on the priest and Mister Rooster began to relax, the Rooster within him crowed, and the noise cut through the still air.

The priest spun around and attempted to locate the Rooster, but none could be seen. He stared out into the assembly, who stared back at him. As the priest attempted to resume his communion, the Rooster cried out again. The priest was mystified,

"Has anybody bought a Rooster to mass this Sunday?" he called out to the villagers who called back that there was a Rooster joining them,

""Where can I find it?" replied the priest calmly. A man quietly stepped up and spoke in his ear,

"The sick person you were looking for is that man with the large belly in the front, there. His belly contains a live Rooster ...who sings ..." The priest stood in silence looking at Mister Rooster for several minutes.

After the mass, the priest approached Mister Rooster and brought him to his home to discuss whether it would be possible to pray for his problem. The walk to the priest's home was very far as he lived outside of the village in a convent where he spends his days among other priests. All of these priests agreed to pray for Mister Rooster, but yet his situation didn't change. After this had failed, they agreed to pay to send Mister Rooster to the hospital so that the specialists could consult with him. He was accompanied by a young priest who brought him to a hospital, which was far from the village and located in the big city. The villagers had a custom of travelling long distances on a trailer packed with possessions and domestic animals. These animals were then sold for money at their destination or traded as payment for accommodation. Mister Rooster got into the vehicle and sat in the cabin next to the driver. Nobody but the young priest knew Mister Rooster's situation; he too was seated by Mister Rooster. An old man hobbled onto the trailer carrying a baby Goat, and the driver paused once more to check that all the passengers had taken their seats before the vehicle pulled off. They set off on the road to the big city, but the roads at that time of year were typically disastrous, where some areas had been cut and maintained for the transport, other areas remained wild and treacherous.

During the dry seasons, the cars ran at high speeds. Yet during these rainy seasons, the water eroded the roads to the point of being almost impossible, leading to journeys taking days instead of hours. At one point as the driver had slowed down on a particularly precarious road, the Rooster began to sing.

Mister Rooster looked across at all of those seated in the vehicle, a woman carried a hen; another man had a pig, but no Roosters.

All of the passengers wondered where this call was coming from. The villagers did not like occurrences which had no obvious explanations as they were deeply moved by ghost stories and superstitions. One by one the passengers' eyes fell on the old man, who was sat next to Mister Rooster as, one at a time, they located where the noise was coming from. Fear was palpable from within the carriage, one woman looked at the old man with the Goat and snarled,

"If you are a wizard, it would be better you get out." To which the old man quickly retorted,

"My Goat does not sing!" At this remark, the vehicle erupted in commotion as each passenger was engulfed in confusion and fear. As Mister Rooster sat quietly, the old man had raised himself up in the brouhaha before landing on his knees in front of Mister Rooster. It was at that moment that the Rooster cried again, those nearby heard it, but were still baffled.

The people paused, focusing on exactly the point where they perceived the noise to come from. The Rooster cried again, right from the Mister Rooster's belly. A young man cursed,

"What kind of magic is this!" While Mister Rooster pretended to drowse to avoid any questions.

Around evening time, the vehicle arrived on the outskirts of the city, where it stopped. The buses would stop here, and families and old friends would run to greet their relatives. The young priest climbed down from the cabin and offered a hand for Mister Rooster to get down with. As all the passengers were now filled with relief after arriving safely at their destinations, they looked at Mister Rooster with pity, now understanding his truth. Small clumps of people formed around the vehicle, discussing Mister Rooster and his mystery. The young man, who had been seated next to Mister Rooster, was greeted by his older brother. Immediately he shared the news about the man with a Rooster in his belly, but his brother stopped him immediately,

"Every time you come home from the village you bring ridiculous stories!" He burst out laughing. At this point, Mister Rooster and the young priest slowly overtook the brothers. The older brother saw Mister Rooster's belly and suggested that it was simply excessive weight gain that he suffered from rather than the fantastic idea that there was a Rooster in his belly.

The brothers walked in the same direction as Mister Rooster who, after a little while, turned to the priest admitting his tiredness and asked if they could sit for a little while. Then the older brother took the opportunity to offer a hand to help the man sit down. As Mister Rooster took the hand, his body relaxed.

The Rooster did not like it when his carrier relaxed his muscles and so let out a large cry. The older brother jumped back and attempted to run away, terrified.

Passers-by and loiterers who witnessed the situation also fled the scene immediately. They feared they would be contaminated, not by any illness, but by bad spirits. Thus, Mr Rooster and the young priest made their way all on their own to the hospital where he was admitted.

Mister Rooster occupied a single room at the hospital. His isolation was mainly in order to avoid the curiosity of other patients and visitors. The doctors did not understand the disease. Nevertheless, they agreed to send him in for an X-ray. Before this, however, the consultant had asked him questions to clarify he was a hermaphrodite and was, in fact, pregnant. One of the first questions asked of him was if he was homosexual. Mister Rooster was horrified. He didn't understand what homosexuality meant! This was common within the villages, though, as the villagers never spoke about same-sex relationships, as the doctor explained, Mister Rooster interjected,

"Am I in a hospital or an asylum for the mentally insane?"
The news arrived at the village that Mister Rooster had been admitted to hospital with the priests. His old friend came to visit him. Mister Rooster's old friend responded to the rumours that the doctors had suggested that he was pregnant,

"What an abomination!" he shouted. "How can a man be pregnant? It must be an evil spirit."

While the two chatted and caught up, one of the doctors approached them with the X-ray results. The doctor described that Mister Rooster had a balloon-like ball in his stomach and that it would be best to operate and remove this ball. Presenting him with a paper, the doctor asked him to sign. Mister Rooster refused initially, demanding that he consult with the priest first.

When the priest entered his room, Mister Rooster begged him to help him leave the hospital and return to the village.

However, the priest calmed him down and discussed the situation with the doctors; they decided that Mister Rooster needed to be transferred to South Africa where there was much more advanced medical technology.

On the day of the transfer, the priest escorted Mister Rooster to the airport.

At security, the young priest wished him a safe journey. Boarding took a very long time. Meanwhile, Mister Rooster was forced to stand upright in a queue for hours, which took a toll on his health.

Finally, Mr Rooster was able to board the aircraft; the people were buzzing about, trying to load all of their luggage in the overhead compartments while Mr Rooster presented his ticket and was shown calmly to his seat. Once seated, Mr Rooster stretched and relaxed, for the journey had been extremely tiring; however, he was very aware that any movement could set the Rooster inside of him off. A man approached the aisle whose seat was on the other side of Mister Rooster and asked him if he would move out of the way. Mister Rooster stirred himself and rose slowly and politely in order to make way for the man, yet at this slight movement, the Rooster sang. There was a silence of breaths. Nobody moved. Not even the air hostess, who stopped dead in the aisle. One passenger turned to her,

"Did you just hear the sound of a Rooster?" to which she replied stone-cold,

"Yes. Yes, I did." She turned towards the aisles and in a stern voice called out, "If anybody has brought a Rooster on this flight, please bring it forward, no animals are allowed on this flight." Her eyes scanned the passengers, and nobody moved a muscle. After a minute of silence, the hostess spun on her heels and trotted off to inform the captain that there was a Rooster on the aircraft.

After a little while, the captain's authoritative, yet slightly irritated voice boomed through the microphone,

"There are no animals allowed on this flight. Not even pets such as Roosters. We have a zero tolerance." However, just as the crackle of the microphone terminated, the Rooster cried again from within Mr Rooster's belly. Heads twitched to and fro while the hostesses darted this way and that, completely baffled by the location of the sound. The man seated next to Mister Rooster pointed the staff to Mister Rooster,

"It is coming from this gentleman; he must be hiding him under his seat!" At this information, the staff and the captain rushed over to Mister Rooster and required him to give away any animal he was concealing under his seat.

Murmurs of disbelief from among the other passengers rose up with whispers such as, "How did he manage that?" and "Unbelievable!"

Mister Rooster pleaded with the captain, "I assure you I have no Rooster."

"Well, then how are we hearing the Rooster's song?" asked the captain. Mister Rooster's face dropped, and with sad eyes, he confessed that the Rooster was in fact in his belly. The murmurs turned into a screeching; the passengers squawked "What an incredible story!" and other statements to the effect of "Bloody Hell!" The captain kept calm but was unsure of what to do. The lady sat behind Mister Rooster refused to travel with him on board, she shared the opinion with some other passengers that having a Rooster within his belly was a sign of sorcery and thus Mister Rooster must be a wizard. The captain concluded and announced to the passengers that having a Rooster within his belly presented no real threat to the other passengers and that therefore the flight could continue uninterrupted. This announcement caused an uproar with one gentleman scoffing, "So if he were just to transform into a Crocodile mid-flight, would that be a threat?" The co-pilot rushed out at this commotion and protested to the captain,

"I know the mentality of these people, keeping him on the plane will cause panic. The best course of action would be to remove him." During these intense deliberations, Mister Rooster had begun to snooze, having been subject to a great deal of stress the past few weeks. He was roused by the captain and co-pilot, informing him that he was to be removed. Mister Rooster, in his dazed state, refused. The woman behind him muttered that it was the nature of a wizard to ignore authority.

It had been an hour, and Mister Rooster still refused to move an inch. The plane awaited the arrival of security who would forcibly remove Mister Rooster from his seat. The news propagated like a puff of smoke; all of the media wrote and spread the story of this commotion. Meanwhile, Mister Rooster was left alone, unsure about where to go.

He was taken into airport security and kept there for quite some time. Soon enough, a pastor walked into the airport and requested that he would deal with Mister Rooster. As security had little idea where to place Mister Rooster, they were happy to pass him over, mindful of the proverb: Every man for himself and God for all.

So, here is how the story of Mister Rooster concludes. The pastor brought Mister Rooster to his church and looked after and prayed for him until he began to recover. The pastor explained to him,

"You simply have a disease caused by the dark magic of wizards. This disease is unable to be cured in hospitals or by modern sciences. It is only by diet and prayers, calling upon the divine power to fight the devilish evil within the victim." He looked kindly at Mister Rooster, "Many people have similar diseases and end their lives not knowing what to do! It is necessary to define the difference between regular diseases caused by biological issues and then of unnatural diseases, of which only the divine powers can destroy."

After only a short amount of time, Mister Rooster, formally known as Bonifacio, was cured and returned joyfully to the village. The church gave him the gift of a bicycle in order to welcome him home. The children of the village did not forget Bonifacio as he rode happily around on his bike, they called out,

"Mr Rooster!"

Chapter 9
Big Boss, the Gorilla

The story which I am going to tell you starts, at first, with the father of the Big Boss, the Gorilla. The father of the Big Boss was the biggest male amongst all of the Gorillas of his generation, which lived in the jungle. In this time, there was a history of poachers who dominated from the village. This was due to a large request for the bones of Gorillas for the manufacture of aphrodisiac products and these bones thus reached a very high price, but why?

According to tradition, the natives used the bones of Gorillas to wash new-born baby boys, while reciting age old incantations. By doing this, the natives hoped the child would grow to be as strong as a Gorilla, become a successful hunter and nourish the family. They say that the Gorilla had only one bone on the forearm similar to a human. However, the human had two.

Another reason why the Gorilla bones were so valued is that, as the human grew older, he became sexually weaker. Then natives used products manufactured with Gorilla bones in order to reactivate the man's sexual force.

If we look at this from another angle, we could appreciate that human behaviour is similar to that of animals; the human male enjoyed having a broad range of sexual partners. It is easy to draw parallels to male Lions dominating and monopolising the young females, and the male Gorilla dominating and monopolising female Gorillas also. For the human males, the older men of the village aspired to have between three and ten women to themselves. If a man only had one woman, he was seen as impotent and weak. However, this number of women required sustained sexual prowess, which, as we have discussed, diminished with age. Therefore, the men of the village often demanded aphrodisiac products in order to maintain their women. The demand opened the market for hunters, who made a lucrative trade from killing Gorillas, the hunters in this trade were referred to as 'poachers'.

The story of the Big Boss begins on the darkest day of his childhood when he witnessed poachers brutally killing his father. The poachers entered his family's home, savagely targeted his mighty and noble father and left the babies and females alone and terrified. This shocking event marked the Big Boss's mind forever. He understood the poaching system well, but even those animals of very limited intelligence knew to flee at the sight of man, it was an innate desire to stay protected from danger.

After seeing his father killed, Big Boss knew he could be killed in this same manner. He was a huge Gorilla just like his father and dedicated his time to preparing the group for protection in the event of poachers. Big Boss thought of an idea that was completely different from all the preceding dominant males; he aimed to build an enclosure. Here is what he planned to do.

From the centre of the closure, there were three paths, which extended to the outside, made secure by the fact that massive tree trunks were suspended by vines above each path. Big Boss would live in the middle of this enclosure where he would spend the nights with his female partners; therefore, if somebody wanted to see Big Boss, it was necessary that his access was authorised. However, if the visit was unauthorised, then the smaller Gorillas detached the tree trunks from the vines, which would squash any intruder. The Big Boss never climbed the trees, but sat, very calmly and pensively, contemplating his offspring, the products of his power. He stayed true to the ancient proverb 'one should not learn the grimaces of the old Gorilla'.

During this time, there was a beautiful girl among the natives named Mahsta.

She was focused and intelligent and insisted on studying within a convent of sisters. However, all her family were against her studious desires as she was so beautiful and nearing the end of her adolescence. This meant that Mahsta had the choice of all men in the village who yearned for her hand in marriage. An elder member of the family had said,

"When you have a beautiful daughter such as Mahsta that means you have found a diamond. The person who finds a diamond keeps it preciously so that one day, that diamond can bring him much wealth." In the same way, having a beautiful girl could also bring wealth to the family by being reserved for the highest bidder. It was for this reason that Mahsta's family were reluctant to allow their diamond out of their sights for they were destitute.

The Chief, named Baptista, of a neighbouring village, a very rich and powerful man, heard the people of his circle speak about a young girl called Mahsta.

After hearing about her extraordinary beauty, the Chief decided to contact her parents and ask them for Mahsta's hand in marriage. In this culture, the bride had no say in who was chosen to be her husband; instead, the parents simply presented the girl to a potential suitor.

Chief Baptista was eighty years old while Mahsta had just turned seventeen, yet age wasn't an influencing factor in the culture regarding marriage as long as the girl was over the age of sixteen. When the news arrived at Mahsta's family that the Chief of a village wanted to marry their daughter, they believed it was the start of the wealth that they had been waiting for. Therefore, knowing the Chief's wealth, they took the opportunity to request an exorbitant dowry of twenty-five cows; this would make them the wealthiest in their village. At times, the family felt remorse over the loss of the daughter, they accepted the revered saying, "You cannot enjoy the honey without enduring the stings of the bees." Chief Baptista accepted the dowry and asked to pay it over two years and, unwilling to miss this opportunity, the family made the deal. Thus, the marriage of Chief Baptista and Mahsta preceded.

During the ensuing days that the couple spent together, their relationship became more problematic. Mahsta understood that the Chief had an issue, and this issue was that Chief Baptista simply did not have the sexual power to satisfy the young girl's needs. Each night, the couple would have a loving conversation before Chief Baptista simply wished her a good night, turned his back, and went to sleep. One day, Mahsta confronted her husband about the problem, and he acknowledged that age had taken its toll; however, he assured her that the issue would be resolved in a few days. How would he find a solution? Baptista consulted his notables for answers, and they recommend that he spoke with the healer. The healer gave Baptista roots and herbs to consume, yet this did nothing to cure his impotence. Another notable had the idea to consult the Tortoise, an ancient and sagacious animal, who had lived through many stories and events and thus may be able to shed a little light on the situation. So, the Tortoise made a formal visit to the Chief on the following evening, surrounded by baffled notables. One of the notables explained the issue fully to the Tortoise who began to laugh uncontrollably at all of the men whom he called ignorant. The Chief grew anxious, this animal was laughing at his vulnerability and thus threatened his authority and Chiefdom.

After recovering from his fit of laughter, the Tortoise said calmly to the Chief, "If the roots that the healers have given you do not work, it is simply because you are too old."

"These kinds of medicines are only effective on those with some strength of youth left within them. Think of it in levels, the men who are lucky with these treatments have, say, level one or two power on their own. Therefore, the treatments are used as an aid. However, in this instance, you have a level zero power. Total impotence." After this explanation, the men broke out in outrage and embarrassment, interjecting the Tortoise and commanding him to solve the issue. In an unaffected tone, the Tortoise continued,

"The only hope is to acquire the testicle of a Gorilla." There was silence. The men looked amongst themselves. Murmuring curses of disbelief and bafflement. "The testicle of a Gorilla will restore your power to the same as it was during puberty." Upon this knowledge, Chief Batista leapt from his seat, "What? You mean to say that I will have the power of my seventeen-year-old self?" He strode about the room excitedly, while the Tortoise smiled wryly.

"The powder created from this ingredient is the most potent remedy of all," he said before leaving to The Griot's hut. The men warned the Tortoise to tell nobody of the information he had heard that day. As he left, they were in awe of how much wisdom a small animal could possess.

That night, the Chief slept with a smile on his lips. He had vivid dreams of how he would take back his power, how he would make love to his wife for the first time, how his life would be different after obtaining that ingredient. When morning broke, the Chief rose with giddiness in his stomach, yet he was unable to share his endeavour with anyone but those in the presence of the former meeting. This was due to the fact that humanitarian forces had begun to crack down to the massacre of jungle animals. Therefore, poachers who were caught in action would be taken to justice courts and tried for their activities. The Chief's men, after reflecting on the words of the Tortoise, began to believe that they too could benefit from the ingredient as well as their master.

The wise Chief addressed these whispers sternly, ordering their patience and obedience as he was the priority. So, the Chief's men recruited five expert hunters and gave them their proposition. The hunters would be provided with spears in order to hunt down a large male Gorilla.

Once this was achieved and brought to the Chief, the hunters would be greatly rewarded and able to keep all of the Gorilla except for his testicles. This included the bones, which would reach a very high price on the black market.

All five hunters, joined by one of the Chief's men and son, who was a keen hunter, accepted this job and began training immediately for their task. This training included target exercises, imitating the throwing of the spear into a Gorilla's heart. From time to time, the hunters would venture out on reconnaissance trips to understand and locate Gorillas in the jungle and decide how they would carry out their attack.

The day of the mission arrived, and the hunters left the village in the very early hours of the morning. The Gorillas were up at these small hours searching for food after a long night. Hardly visible in the thick fog of dawn, the hunters crept quietly through the jungle, only the faraway cries of Birds could be heard. The strategy was that upon their arrival at the Gorilla's territory, they would imitate Gorilla war cries, encouraging the beasts to meet them. Usually, at this sign of danger, the female and infant Gorillas would flee and seek safety, leaving the dominant males to confront the threat. However, this time, something was very different. When the hunters hollered their war cries, they observed that the young males ran, not towards them as expected, but up to the treetops, much like the females and infants would. The hunters found this reaction deeply suspicious but followed the path, which they had seen a young male take. They walked vigilantly and wearily in single-file, watching and scanning for dominant males. Suddenly, as if dropped from the heavens, an enormous tree-trunk, weighing more than six hundred kilogrammes, fell and killed the first three hunters. Horrified, the two hunters behind them tried to escape but it was too late, another massive trunk crushed them also.

Only the sixth had escaped the falling tree trunks, and he attempted to help his companion, who was struggling to breathe but was alive, wedged between the two trees. However, he just wasn't strong enough to lift the trunk before the male Gorillas rained down like bullets from the sky. The sixth hunter saw the dominant male hurtling towards him from a distance and decided to preserve his life by fleeing as far away as he could. As he moved away, his companion grabbed his foot,

"If we die, we all die." The howling of the dominant male grew louder and louder while the hunter struggled with incredible force to free himself. Just as he had managed to break free and spring off into the trees, Big Boss stood upright in front of his companion.

He moved towards the man pressed between the two trunks, Big Boss wedged his huge hands between the trees and pulled back the immense trunk, freeing the hunter. The man stood frozen in his wake, sure of his certain death.

Dropping to his knees, he shut his eyes and awaited his fate.

Big Boss saw blood running down the hunter's arm, he touched it gently, feeling the hot texture of blood. After seeming to ponder on his wound, Big Boss turned on his heel and left with no malice. The hunter opened his eyes after a long time, only to find that the huge Gorilla was no longer there. The survivor ran and ran, with the fear of death in his feet, until he came to rest in his hut. The people of the village saw him running and began to follow him.

They called his name but he refused to speak. When he had rested enough, the survivor summoned up the courage to tell the Chief the news. He explained in details the events that occurred in the jungle, but on hearing the account, the Chief threw a fit and was later pronounced dead.

After the Chief had died, Mahsta arranged her luggage and prepared to return to her parents. However, the young nephew of the Chief refused to allow her departure. The late Chief's nephew insisted that Mahsta remains under the marital roof, this shocked those who overheard. How could he maintain the idea that Mahsta was bound to the conjugal roof after her husband had died?

The nephew replied to these objections stating,

"As my great uncle had no sons, it is only right that I take over his property. This includes his wife."

The law stated that only the brother of the deceased could inherit a wife. However, the brother of the Chief, much like the Chief was extremely old and suffered the same impotence as his late brother. He had heard of the tragic struggle to obtain the remedy and for this reason refused to take Mahsta as his wife. Therefore, Mahsta's family were astonished at the nephew's proclamation and agreed that he could have Mahsta only if he promised to take on the remaining payments, which consisted of ten cows. The nephew could not pay this debt, and thus, Mahsta was returned home with the same purity which she left with. This persevering virtuousness labelled her with the nickname, 'The Blessed Girl'.

Upon hearing about the story of Big Boss and his exploits, a humanitarian, The Griot, two Europeans and some animals formed a group and decided to pay a visit to Big Boss.

The objective of this visit was to convince Big Boss to relocate his band of Gorillas to Virunga Park, where they would be protected from poachers. They aimed to inform him about the peaceful and friendly nature of the park where all were respected equally and where men could not harm them. Despite their words, Big Boss refused,

"Man never holds his word. His mind is so weak that a fly may land on him and he changes it." With that ominous remark, he sloped behind his hut, leaving his guests alone for a minute. There were three chairs where the guests stood, one in the middle and two by the side. Big Boss did not ask his guests to sit. For the Gorillas, those who sat on the chairs were more powerful than those who stood or sat upon the ground. Therefore, the guests were perched on the floor while Big Boss was seated. Sula Cointer, who was one of the group, took the opportunity of Big Boss's absence to sit on one of the prestigious chairs. He giggled while the rest of the guests gasped and hissed at him to get back to the floor. All were silent as they heard the heavy footsteps of

Big Boss from around the hut, Sula leapt off the chair. As he threw himself back to the floor, though, the chair swivelled slightly to the side. Big Boss's great shadowy figure entered the hut and paused; his large amber eyes fixated on the chairs. Quickly his temper shot to the skies,

"Somebody has sat on my chair, which means someone wants to challenge my power!" The Gorilla stood tall and beat his great fists upon his very solid chest.

The chair Sula Cointer had sat upon was Big Boss's and was coloured red at the feet. The guests were backed up into the corner by Big Boss's terrifying display of fury; The Griot took the initiative and lay down on the ground slowly, requiring Big Boss to calm himself, others followed suit. Big Boss glared at each visitor, in turn, spitting out every word with contempt,

"I will kill the bastard who dared to challenge me." Sula Cointer, needless to say, soiled his breeches at this display of terrifying malice. The Griot coolly and gently lifted his head,

"Big Boss, you are the most powerful being in this jungle, there is no doubt. Yet you are mistaken, the wind caused one of the chairs to fall, and we only replanted it randomly. That is all that occurred here." The Griot cooed and was supported by the group, relieved at the hope of safety. Thus, Big Boss calmed down, but he noted the cold, dark stain on Sula Cointer's breeches and his deep chuckles vibrated the walls of the hut. The group joined Big Boss's laughter and left shortly after.

When an animal killed a man, there were always cries. When a man killed an animal, the business occurred in silence, and not much was spoken about it. The Gorilla's massacre of the hunters was spoken about heroically by some who donned him with the nickname Big Boss. As the Lion was king of the animals according to legend, the Gorilla was the owner of the animals in the jungle. The two animals lived in very different territories, with the Lion in the savannah and the Gorilla in the jungle. The Lion often made fun of the Gorilla as he nourished himself on leaves and fruits like the lowest of beings while the Lion indulged on the fresh meats of animals that he kills, thus demonstrating his superiority as king.

The heroism of the Gorilla created a vengeful sentiment within the village. The humanitarians and pacifists amongst the people tried to explain that the Gorilla never encroached into the village in order to kill humans. Rather, the Gorilla was a peaceful animal, who only responded to humans' provocation. However, the issue was that due to the top-secret nature of the Chief's mission, many of the people were not aware of the brutal nature of the hunter's trek into the jungle.

Thus, they believed the attack was malicious, with only the surviving hunter and a very few of the late Chief's men knowing the truth.

The humanitarians and those respectful of nature believed the fundamental truth that the agreement between man and animal must be based on a principle of non-negotiable and reciprocal respect of territory. That was why the people agreed on becoming 'Generation Wild'. This title meant that the behaviour of the villagers based on the old belief superstitions had to be abolished. Africa had five large animals that fell victim to these traditions: The Lion, the Gorilla, the Leopard, the Elephant and the Rhinoceros. The Lion was slaughtered for his bones, of which people believed recovered ferocity, while his gums were valuable in order to make amulets and both reached a very high price on the market. The Gorilla was killed for his bones and teeth; these were often used for medicines against impotence. The Leopard was hunted for the beauty of his skin, often used to create camouflage for soldiers or worn by leaders to signify power. The Elephant was murdered for ivory, a very profitable trade for jewellery and artefacts. Finally, the Rhinoceros was slaughtered for his horn, often referred to as his missile, and used as a symbol of danger which was attached to houses, door or placed in homes.

We are 'Generation Wild' and say no to the unnecessary murder of animals.

Chapter 10

Pedro Navarro, the Elephant

In the small hours of the morning, when they had no food in the house, the natives ventured into the jungle to look for nourishment. In contrast, the townsmen would go to the supermarket for their provisions. The difference here was that the townsmen needed money to buy their food while the natives needed a machete or arrows to catch their dinner or a small bag to gather insects.

One morning, Michael Comma, the hunter, was hiking when he came across a baby Elephant, who had been abandoned by his mother. Michael discovered that his mother was only a little distance away but was dying and unable to move. On seeing this, Michael had sorrow in his heart and pity for the infant.

He thought to himself, *I can't give up this baby, or else it will become prey for wild animals.* After a little thinking, Michael took the baby Elephant as his own and away from the incapable care of his mother. However, the glance of the mother reflected a feeling of compassion as if to urge the man to look after her offspring. On this sight, Michael took the baby home and began to nourish him.

Michael was poor and had difficulty feeding the small Elephant. He had to find food for his family, as well as the infant and his wife was not happy watching the Elephant consuming all of the food that could be keeping her children healthy. The longer the Elephant stayed at home, the more displeased she became. His wife tried to convince Michael to sell the animal, however, Michael was deeply opposed to the idea, and despite his lack of means, he managed to keep the Elephant and his family fed.

The baby Elephant grew and grew, and so did his ivory tusks. The idea of selling the Elephant remained in Michael's wife's head, especially with the increase of ivory consumption within the villages. By looking at the Elephant, she could see easily that he could be sold at a very high price. Michael was disgusted at the idea and could not be convinced. The Elephant now became very friendly, with Michael providing him food daily before bringing him along to help plough the fields. It was not astonishing in this village that people liked to live with animals, and at home, the Elephant could even be found playing with the children of the village. When it rained, water flooded the river, which separated the two villages; people had great difficulty crossing the river without becoming drenched.

The flooding lasted several days, and some adults started to pay to cross the river on the back of this Elephant. They paid in money or nature, Michael collected the cash, and this business became very lucrative for his family, allowing him to live prosperously. The Elephant saw this work as a sort of game, after eating well and being satisfied, he would go to the river and carry people on his back under the watchful eye of Michael who sat and counted the money. In the evening, they would return home; the money had allowed Michael to buy more land and cultivate his fields. This was how a once poor man became rich thanks to his trusting Elephant. Now his wife treated the Elephant in a decent way due to the wealth that he had brought.

After the rainy season, it was time for the dry season. Yet, the Elephant didn't remain inactive. He worked with Michael in the fields. The Elephant ploughed the field while Michael cultivated the maize, which was also referred to as groundnut.

Using the Elephant to plough the field was a significant advantage as it allowed Michael to produce a lot more product as opposed to the other men, who had only their axes and hands to harvest their crops. Eventually, Michael Comma became a wealthy man who provided the most produce in the village and the surrounding area.

The fully-grown male Elephant was given the name 'Pedro Navarro, the Elephant'. Michael Comma benefitted from the strength of Pedro the Elephant and was regarded as the richest man in the village. However, he was seen in a bad light by the Chief and his notables and was given the name 'The New Rich Man' as his money was gained through business instead of being born into riches. He walked with his hand in his pocket, and when greeted, he answered with arrogance. Did his wealth make this difference? When he was questioned about why he always put his hand in his pocket, Michael would answer that it was a sign of wealth because any poor man had nothing to present. This arrogant spirit and money compelled Michael to apply for a position as a notable in the village. This position was regarded as a representative of the villagers who remained near the Chief, something similar to a deputy prime minister. He started corrupting his fellow members by offering them his produce or by buying their trust in order to be elected as a notable. However, the Chief and the current notables did not appreciate Michael's activities.

Furthermore, most notables came from noble families, but Michael was born as a poor man. For these reasons, the notables started to ponder on ways to stop him from succeeding, but on the other hand, the fanaticism of the villagers regarding Michael grew and grew.

After some reflection, the notables realised that the Elephant was the source of all of Michael's wealth. The only way to stop Michael's growing riches was to get rid of the Elephant. They came up with an excuse to separate the two, stating that an Elephant was not a pet and must be freed instead of working in the field. With this reasoning in mind, they created a fake document to convince Michael, who was uneducated and illiterate, that he must let go of Pedro the Elephant.

Michael comma had a nephew who went to school a long way away in another village. In his class, when the teacher read out a passage, he would call out the punctuation, always putting "full stop!" at the end of each sentence. When his uncle Michael visited, he would always make fun of him because his name was 'Comma'. The Chief and his notables called Michael to their building in order to sign the fake document with the supervision on their solicitor from the city.

This solicitor was the man who constructed the false document. However, Michael refused to sign a document as he didn't understand how to sign his name, so he wanted to see his little nephew, who was called, to consult him on signing the document. His little nephew laughed when confronted, and simply taught his uncle how to write a comma.

The following day, Michael returned to the men who presented him with the document.

"This document will give you full responsibility regarding the animal." The solicitor laid the paper in front of Michael and pointed to the place where he was supposed to sign. Michael simply put a comma on the dotted line before sending the document back.

"Sir? Sorry, you didn't sign your name, I can only see a comma."

Michael smiled, "What do you see?"

"Just a comma!" the solicitor replied.

"My name is Michael Comma, that comma is my signature," Michael told the men.

The solicitor looked at the Chief before advising him that the document would not be valid with this signature and doesn't represent a thing. Yet Michael could not be persuaded that this comma could not be used as a signature.

At this time, all of the hunters in the village and the surrounding area were looking around to find a baby Elephant for themselves. They wished to imitate Michael's rise to wealth and fame.

Most of the villagers were tagalongs who got by imitating those who were successful. However, Michael was lucky to have found Pedro Navarro in that situation, as no animals would typically allow a human to take their child away from them. But because Navarro grew up with Michael nurturing him, he accepted the habits of humankind and put his strength to any task that his master gave him.

In the end, the notables, the solicitor, and the Chief agreed that the comma could represent Michael Comma's name and the matter was settled. Michael Comma began to regret not learning to read or write, even though he was rich, he was still illiterate. The situation that Michael found himself in was experienced by many villagers, and it was for that reason that many avoided going to the big city. These people preferred to remain in their corner of the bush and lived together with animals. At least in comparison to the animals, they felt superior.

The news circulated the village that Michael would no longer possess the Elephant, which soon arrived at Michael's own ears. On hearing these allegations, Michael requested to see the Chief in order to understand what was going on. The Chief explained to him that the animal was not a pet and was to be freed.

Michael's heart dropped in surprise. Usually, if a person doesn't accept the rulings of a Chief, the notables come together and decide the course of action. But Michael was sure that the notables would not do anything to contradict the Chief, so he returned home to think more about his predicament.

The truth was that the Chief and his notables didn't want the presence of Michael Comma in residence, but now he was no longer the owner of the Elephant, the Elephant was to be handed to Virunga Park where he would live in peace. Unfortunately, Pedro Navarro refused to leave his master, Michael, because, for him, work was like a game. He loved living stress free, working at what he was good at and eating well. The transporters that the Chief had called for were too afraid to hustle the animal because if angered, Pedro Navarro could cause catastrophic damage. Therefore, they left the animal alone and reported the happenings to the Chief. Michael too returned to the Chief to argue that he was indeed the rightful owner of the Elephant and nobody else had a right to take him away. In response, the Chief showed Michael the document that he had signed stating that Michael would give up the animal.

Michael didn't understand, the document being shown to him was the same one which he thought would allow him to become a notable. He felt as if the sky was falling on his shoulders, and he returned home to reflect. How could he prevent this plot from unfolding? This was a knife in his back as all the notables stood behind the Chief on this evil plan.

The Chief had arranged that some animals come and convince Pedro Navarro to live in the park with them. Among these animals were the Chimpanzee, a giraffe, another Elephant who were already friends of Pedro. The Chimpanzee was now very close to the Elephant because he had heard of the work that the Elephant did when carrying people on his back across the river. The Chimpanzee, who was very malicious, wanted to continue this business with the Elephant. As we all know, Chimpanzees love to eat bananas. However, the villagers monopolised the area where the banana trees grew in order to sell them. For this reason, the animals, including Chimpanzees, found it difficult to find bananas for themselves. The Chimpanzee did not want to miss an opportunity to use this Elephant to gain wealth, which he could use to buy his preferred fruits. The Chimpanzee visited the Tortoise to convince the Elephant to move into the park and stop working for the humans.

During the rainy season, the Chimpanzee and the Elephant began to work together. The Elephant continued his old job of transporting people across the river while the Chimpanzee received payment. The two animals began to make a lot of money, so much so that some villagers became jealous of their success. However, the problem arose when it came to women, more specifically, pregnant women. The pregnant women did not trust the face of the Chimpanzee to take care of them and their babies. They began to fear that their children would be born with the face of a Chimpanzee. Finally, they asked if the Chimpanzee could give this job to his brother as they did not wish to see his face each day.

"Who is my brother?" questioned the Chimpanzee. The women replied that the Monkeys were his brothers.

"No way! The Monkeys have tails – I haven't!" he protested.

However, the women continued, "The cat has their big brother, the Leopard, who often helps them out. Who is your brother then if it isn't the Monkeys?"

The Chimpanzee looked at them and said, "Humans are my brothers."

The men around them didn't accept this response. One man opened his shirt to the level of his chest and spat saliva on his chest, swearing that he would never be the brother of a Chimpanzee. The villagers spit on their chest as a symbol of disrespect, often swearing against whatever phenomena had provoked their disgust.

This habit of spitting on their chest and swearing was a hurdy-gurdy habit. Many albino individuals faced this behaviour and confrontation regularly. People who cross albinos in the street often spit on their chest and declared, "Never will an albino be born into my family," or simply turn their head to the side and mutter, "I didn't see you." Many young girls who saw an albino in the distance would take long detours as not to walk near them. As they changed direction, they spat on their chests and denounced the albino; for example, many spat and hissed, "I will never give birth to an albino." This spitting was a superstition, which was meant to protect them against the atrocity before their eyes. That was why the men spat in response to the Chimpanzee's statement.

As the new generation, we must fight against this mentality. Many healers have made albinos out to be devils as they do not understand the phenomena.

To keep their customers under the impression that they were all-knowing, they told lies describing the albinos as witches. Today we are aware of the truth that albinos are ordinary people like everyone else. That is why, as the new generation, we must fight for a rebirth of mentality, one which respects all animals and fellow humans.

A man from the village was reported missing and was discovered deep in Virunga Park; he told the authorities that the Elephant belonged to him,

"If you want to recover an animal, why are you going so deep into the park?" they asked him coolly, to which Michael Comma stated that he had found a female Elephant that Navarro could marry and begin a family with.

"Unfortunately, we cannot let you do this, we have a document from the Chief stating that we have the right to keep the Elephant here." However, Michael rejected this document by shouting that the document was fraudulently made by the Chief and his notables with intent to take his Elephant from him. On these words, the authorities called the Chief as they could not enforce laws with a fraudulent document.

The Chief was very annoyed at this inconvenience and presented the papers to the authorities and demonstrated where Michael Comma had signed the document. However, Michael saw this opportunity,

"Look! I only put a comma, that's not my name." However, the notables supported the Chief in this matter. However, Michael jumped at their argument,

"I only put a comma, and I didn't even put a full stop. To finish a sentence, you need a full stop!"

The Chief put both of his hands on his head and muttered under his breath,

"This man is a swindler." His notables stood puzzled at Michael's grammatical knowledge as they were sure he was illiterate.

The park's authorities were unsure how to decide, but this news reached the ears of Master Tortoise Bonaventure, the lawyer of Virunga Park. The Tortoise told Michael that he had finished his exploitation of the animal and now the animal, being an adult, didn't depend on anybody and nobody had the right to assign him a female partner, that an adult animal could decide this himself.

"You must leave here and forget about that Elephant," he said looking into Michael's eyes. The authorities of the park enforced the Tortoise's orders.

On his turning away, all of the animals rejoiced, except for Master Tortoise.

Later, upon reflection, Master Tortoise Bonaventure wrote a letter to the United Nations. He showed the letter to all of the animals to gain their support. The purpose of the letter was to draw attention from the international authorities regarding the fate of animals. It was worded as follows:

Mr General Secretary of the United Nations.
Dear Sir,

I am writing to you in the name of all animals to bring your attention to their fate.

Each day the animals are killed and maltreated by man, either to be eaten or sold to the black market for skins, ivory or painful labour. Thus, I raise the alarm to your worldwide organisation.

We require that all animals must be respected and protected from human violence.

We propose the creation of an international agency, which will deal with this protection and a creation of green spaces where we can live in peace. Endorsement of our cause and an encouragement of man to digest this message would be greatly appreciated.

Kind Regards,
Master Tortoise Bonaventure. Lawyer of all animals.

Chapter 11

The King Lion and the Queen Lioness

The Hegemonya was all the time, an act of supremacy to dominate his fellow man or one tribe to dominate another. The villagers who form a village, in the majority of the cases came from the same tribe. And there were always fights; fratricides between two tribes because one wanted to have more power than the other.

We saw in one of the chapters: the case of one of the tribes, the Lions, which got dressed with the mask of the Lion, trying to impose its law on other tribes.

So, others didn't oppose their ideas and never stole their goods. They made other rival tribes to believe that they could send a Lion during the night to devour them when they had a problem with them. This superstition was inculcated in the memory of other tribes and they were afraid of the hegemonya or predominance of the Lion tribe. Only the Hyenas, regarded as brigand animals, had breached this belief whilst stealing the meat of the Lion tribe. If an individual sought to dominate fellow members, he could be qualified as a dictator. We saw in the life of human beings some Chiefs acting as dictators and also in the animal life such as the Gorillas; with the male dominating the group or a group of Lions. This kind of domination forced the leaders to show that they had the capacity to dominate. In the animals it was the force of the male, which dominated; in the man it was the intelligence and the power. Thus, the human leaders or the dominating males wanted to have power to manage their people.

The King Lion wanted to have advice and went to consult the Tortoise, the most respected, wisest animal. The King Lion did not want to withdraw from the pleasure, which the monarchy offered him. He had priority to change female partners as he wanted. The woman Lioness offered food to him each day. Being the king, he could not be driven out. But on the other side, he saw a bad effect of the resurgence of the young males; something should be done.

The Tortoise, especially advised him not to eat the Tortoise because he was a sacred animal, which had a long life compared to other animals. The idea not to eat the flesh of the Tortoise remained accepted till now. The Lion never liked to taste the flesh of the Tortoise because of the allegation. The Tortoise gave him the example of his cousin, the marine Tortoise, which lived more than 150 years. He advised the King Lion not to couple with the old women, because they bring the curse, while the young women, especially virgins, bring blessings and endurance. The Tortoise's advice did not only apply to animals as even humans regard these as truth. When a man gets old, especially the tribes' Chiefs, they like to get married again with a young girl to invigorate themselves physically and spiritually. And, also, the villagers maintained that a man must get married with a younger woman because while becoming old, the woman would have the energy and also be able to care for her husband. Whereas if the couple were of the same age, on getting old, the woman would be unable to care for her husband and the husband would be unable to care for his wife. This is because both would be old. That's why villagers liked to get married with young beautiful girls.

The King Lion was very happy and convinced on hearing Tortoise's advice. That is why, whilst returning back home, the King Lion started to plan to dispatch the Queen Mother, who had started to get old because she could bring curses in his life. He started to avoid even coupling with the Queen Lioness. Being the dominating male, he coupled now only with the youngest Lioness. The Queen Mother did not understand why she was scorned by her husband. This act to scorn your spouse also exists in human beings. Many women suffered from the bad behaviour of men. Men set up the polygamy in their life to hide the bad intention towards women and also the submission of women as housewives.

Now would the Queen Mother accept this behaviour?

Currently, the new generation is opposed to this bad behaviour towards women. It is an act of benevolence. This act must also continue by protecting animals by banishing the exploitation of the animals and the consumption of the animal flesh.

The Queen Lioness finally understood the problem and sought now to eliminate all rivals. She did not want to let herself be manipulated by the King's ideas.

Being the Queen Lioness, she needed to act. All the young female Lionesses who would approach the King would be her adversaries. As the woman went to hunt and get food for the King, the Queen Lioness, a very wild and experienced woman would benefit from the occasion to eliminate her rival during the hunt. She trailed her rival in an ambush and killed her. But after three of his co-inhabitants were killed, the King Lion started to have suspicions. Now all his new conquests were dying by accidental death during hunting because that was the explanation which the Queen Lioness gave, but the King was not convinced. The villagers said that women have very developed wisdom, that men were not aware of. A woman could mislead her husband easily without the man being aware. Thus, the natives introduced into their habitat a mystical ceremony, which consists of making the woman swear to be faithful to her husband. In the case of disobedience, the woman would suffer the death penalty. This mentality came into force when one of the Chiefs had several women and the youngest carried out to go out with her lover. By discovering the case, it was a dishonour to the Chief. Then, to remedy this situation, all men had decided to create this mystical ceremony before the wedding.

Finally, the King Lion conquered a young beautiful Lioness and decided to stay with her all the time. There was no question that she had to go and hunt with the others. The Queen Mother, as usual, objected to this idea because she didn't want to risk her life by hunting to get food for another woman. This trend of the Queen to oppose against her husband was not recent because women had always had the energy to oppose against the stupidity of the men. In the same way, the native women in the past also had the energy to oppose the incision of young girls. Themselves being incised in their youth, they wanted to avoid this suffering to their children. The custom required this incision always with the idea to keep women faithful to her husband. When becoming a mother, women were opposed to this act because they said the act caused unnecessary suffering that did not prevent them from disobedience. According to the women, it was not the incision that could stop them from disobeying.

The solution was to leave the village that practiced this act and seek a better place. Then men started to note the spontaneous departure of many women, fleeing this dastardly act and abolished the incision of the young girls. In fact, we don't know where the practice of incision came from; a creation from men, said some women. On the other side, the circumcision of young boys is biblical, an act enacted by God himself, following the bible of Christians. Even some religions such as Muslims practice circumcision, and it is regarded as a normal act. Because the young boy, when grown up, appreciates this act, unlike the young girl, who rejects the incision. If men always tend to manipulate women, it's only to satisfy their sexual appetite. This concept also applies to male animals.

The Chief, who was married to the young girl, did not know that the young girl had a lover. The young boy was called Mario. He was in love with the young girl since young age. The young girl, being married, didn't want to give up her young lover because this marriage with the old Chief was not her intention.

Mario always lived with his parents and from Chief's house the young bride had to cross in front of Mario's family home on her way to visit her parents.

From time to time, after cooking good food, the young girl asked the Chief to allow her to take some food to her father, who was already old. *Normal idea to help her parents,* the Chief thought, but the girl, on her way, stopped at her lover's house and the food was not intended for her father but for Mario, her lover. Even the money that the young girl received from her husband, was intended for Mario. Mario always dressed very well compared to the other boys in the village. Even the Chief himself appreciated Mario and said, "This boy is very smart and worthy of the village."

Considering the poverty, some young girls were confronted often with this kind of problem. It happened that a young girl would go out with an old man, but this was not due to love but rather for her to take money from their pockets. Because it was not by love that she was going out with the old man but because of her financial situation; she had no choice.

On the other side, the old man, very obsessed by sex benefitted from this youth and called them 'sweetheart', unaware that he was being used.

That's one of the reasons they had created the mystical ceremony. Some tribes called this ceremony 'TSHIBAWU'.

In the case of the Chief, the day he discovered that his money was going straight to Mario, he was filled with rage and decided to separate with his young spouse.

The Chief bought a compound to build a new house and put it in the name of his new spouse. He advised his young spouse that he would build a house for her and their child, which would be born from their union. But later, people from the land register informed the Chief that there was an unknown name listed as an owner. And this name was the name of Mario. After enquiries, the secret connection with the lover was revealed. The handsome young man whom the Chief appreciated was only his rival, and the lover of his wife. Everyone in the village knew about this affair, except the Chief and his notables. The woman was now pregnant, and the people wondered if the baby was from the Chief or from Mario.

The King Lion wanted to impose his new mistress like queen. Unfortunately, this was unacceptable for the old queen, who claimed her right of birth and as a queen couldn't be dethroned in one click. Usually the queen could be dethroned or the king in the event of failure to her rights or for the queen in the event of adultery. But that's not the case actually; The King wanted only to satisfy his sexual appetite and to apply the advice given to him by the Tortoise, because the Queen Mother was already an old woman.

The King Lion once again went to consult the Tortoise, to ask for advice. But the Tortoise indicated to him of the big witchcraft in the village, which would be able to help him. But while returning, a young male came to impose in front of the King Lion and his guards and declared to fight with the King. What disobedience! The young male was not happy with the King because his female partner had gone to join the group of young girls who surrounded the King.

Thus, the young male was very annoyed because the King was taking all the young females. He presented himself in front of the King and decided to fight him. In this situation, if the young male beat the King and killed him, he would automatically become king. Otherwise, he would be killed by the guards if the King wins. The King's guard knew the young male very well and they wanted to fight and kill him. But the King asked them to leave him; he would fight with the young male to prove that he was a brave king and was not scared of anything. Due to this fact, the guards left free ground to both belligerents. The guards of the King were convinced that their brave warrior king would kill his adversary. But what they were unaware of was that the King was also old and too much sex with the young Lionesses had weakened him. The king spent his time eating and making love. The battle was hard and the confrontation was going in favour of the young male. The Queen, seeing that, asked herself a question, *If this young male wins, I will not be a queen,* then she intervened and killed the young Lion.

After the battle, the King noted that he was in danger with the insurgence of the young male. He thought that he had to show he had the capacity to control his people. He had to show his people that he was a powerful king, because the approach of the young male put the King in doubt about his ability to control the group. To calm the young males, the King decided to stop having affairs with all the females; but instead chose three young females who would be his partners. He went to consult the witchcraft of the Tortoise. Because the Tortoise considered that the current situation of the King Lion deserved intervention of a big wizard.

The King Lion said, "That's a good idea. All good leaders aspire to dominate their people by controlling them well."

The King Lion went to see the wizard. The wizard welcomed them, the King and his two soldiers, who were bodyguards. This visit was normal, especially for the animals, and the natives who lived far away from modern civilisation. In the event of an insolvent problem, it was necessary to consult a person who had supernatural power and this person was the wizard.

The wizard explained to the King and his girlfriends that he would be killed because his accomplices were not afraid of him.

"They want to discover if you are really a powerful king," the wizard said. He said that that he was the only person who could make the King very powerful and everyone would be afraid of him, including other animals.

The King Lion shook his head by looking at one of his bodyguards and said, "That's the truth, because without power, how can a leader control his people?"

The wizard prepared the King that he was going to make incantations to make him invincible to any temptation or plot; and he was going to dominate all his fellow members and he would restore his power. But also, it was necessary to invent a history which would make his fellow citizens afraid.

The wizard proposed to the king that his soldiers would return home, and announce that the King was dead following a disease that the wizard could not cure. Afterwards, they would bring an empty coffin which they would bury, pretending that the king was inside. After three days, the King would reappear wearing all white clothes, to make the people believe that the king had been resurrected.

Everyone would be afraid, and he would become a very powerful king.

The soldiers of the king created a coffin and put an animal inside with some trunk of a tree so that the coffin would be heavy like the weight of a Lion. Initially, the king sent one of his soldiers to send back the message that the king Lion had passed away following a disease that the wizard could not cure. Everyone knew that the king was on a trip. When the news arrived; all the group were sad for the loss of their leader. And the soldier announced that the body of the king would be brought back tomorrow for burial. As announced, the following day, the soldiers brought back the coffin and all the community were shocked to see the coffin. The queen mother received the coffin with the soldiers who were back up remaining with her. Very sceptic, the queen mother announced to the community that she wanted to see the body of her husband before being buried. The soldiers who brought the coffin opposed the queen's idea, saying that it was the wish of the king to be buried in a coffin and nobody could say no! The coffin was in the middle, the queen and the soldiers on one side and the soldiers on the other side. The crowd also followed the scene; everyone was quiet because the king was dead. At a stretch the queen still took the speech by saying that the king was now dead, but while waiting to establish another king, it was her who would decide now. The sixth sense of the queen told her that there was something of a hurdle. It raised the question, why the soldiers would not open the coffin? The queen still took the floor by saying that she must see the body of her husband before he was buried. But the soldiers of the king again opposed and words were exchanged between the queen and the soldiers. The scenario started to take an unpleasant aspect. The soldiers insisted that the body of the king must be respected and not be exposed to everyone. Then the queen sent one of her soldiers to open the coffin, only for the queen to see the body of her husband. The king's soldiers opposed again, and a brawl burst out between the two parties. The situation had become unbearable and some animals began to flee. The queen with a dash, raised the coffin with the help of one of her soldiers and threw the coffin to the ground. The coffin opened and the brawl stopped… And everyone with astonishment noted that the king was not inside. Upon seeing that the secrecy was revealed, the soldiers of the king ran away in the direction towards the king to tell him that the business did not work.

Here was how the reign of the Queen Mother started. The King Lion was declared as a prohibited man in the community, and regarded as an imposter. The Queen Mother dethroned the king of his functions. The faithful of the King and his girlfriends were sacked from the community. There were now two tribes, one controlled by the Queen and the other controlled by the unfortunate King.

The King and his soldiers and some of his sympathisers went to live very far away from the clan of the Queen to avoid confrontation. Two soldiers of the King were very annoyed with the wizard of the village and went during the night to kill him. Because they thought the wizard made them swallow the poison. Because of him, they were now in misfortune. But the King Lion didn't think the same as his soldiers. For the King, it was the silly female, the Queen who was promoter of their misfortune because the wizard had a good idea. However, one day it would be avenged against his advocate, the Queen. According to the nature, never should one lie to the wild animals because they were vindictive and nasty. The first night that the King spent out of his community, he howled in the night and all the animals, which lived in the surrounding, were afraid. Because when the King of the animals howled, it meant that there was a problem. Two clans broke up, born regarded as brothers, now enemies.

While in other clans, no one howled because it was a woman who was on the throne. That made the difference.

Chapter 12

Buffalo, the Raffish Animal

The Buffalo was an animal who behaved differently from his herbivorous accomplices. Usually, the herbivorous animals such as the Antelope, Zebra, the giraffe, were flexible and non-aggressive. But the Buffalo, considering his weight and his size, differed from the others; very malicious and aggressive. The Buffalo always wanted to dominate and to impose hiss point of view onto others.

In the event of disobedience, he used the force without pity towards the villainous ones. Many of his accomplices did not like to cohabitate with him and avoid his presence in all circumstances. But this time, Buffalo had somebody to share time with. It was the Antelope, who was a very intelligent animal like the Tortoise, and was especially very astute and trick. If the Buffalo tried to handle the Antelope, he always found a way to avoid him. The place where the Buffalo lived was very bushy. And many herbivores were attracted by the presence of these green sheets that the Buffalo regarded as private property. He approached him and created a friendship. Where the Buffalo lived, the other animals avoid approaching or to pass near the place because if the Buffalo caught you, you would be forced to pay an infringement. Any animal had the right to own his ground. In the event of refusal, you were likely to have a blow of hooves or a massive blow of horns. Then many animals understood and they tried to avoid approaching the Buffalo. While being with him; Buffalo always sought a service for his well-being or to make harm to others.

Here's how the Buffalo, the Raffish lives. And he said it was in the name of the Buffalo, do this or do that. It was not for nothing he was called the Raffish. It acted for his well-being and wanted others to satisfy his desire. As the other animals avoided attending Buffalo, Antelope had preferred to mix with this mastodon, even with his foul temper. His goal was to find protection near the brother Buffalo.

The Antelope, was an animal without force and also the prey of other animal forces. The only factor which enabled him to be protected in the event of aggression, was to escape. But while being held concurrently to the Buffalo, no animal would come to attack him, by fear of being thrashed by the Buffalo, and especially, also to profit from the green grass which flooded around the Buffalo's place. It was a tip that many animals used to be protected from the strongest. Thus, the small fish swam on the side of the shark, to protect itself from large fish, who were afraid of the shark.

In his dimension, the Buffalo had accepted the presence of the Antelope because it profited to eat some leaves unknown in his menu. Buffalo was only satisfied with the leaves or grass which grow around his ground. He did not have the courage to make a long way to seek other grass or leaves like Antelope made. Whereas Antelope, as small as he was, very nimble, ran a long way and brought back different sheets to vary the menu. The day Antelope brought some sweet potato to Buffalo, he was very content with this friend because he ate well with appetite. Buffalo benefited from food that Antelope brought to him, and Antelope benefited from the protection of the Buffalo.

Both made a good couple of friends and they understood each other very well.

One day, the Antelope brought maize and started to eat alone, without sharing with Buffalo. Buffalo was curious and asked his friend what he was eating. The Antelope told him that he was eating the beautiful teeth of his mother.

Buffalo was astonished and asked the Antelope, "How can you eat the teeth of your mother?"

The Antelope told him that you must boil the teeth until they were soft and ready to eat. As Buffalo did not know the maize and never ate this vegetable, he did not understand. But when he tasted the maize, it was soft and succulent, and Buffalo was thinking how the teeth could be so succulent. He already thought to kill his mother and to taste this marvellous vegetable. But Buffalo, still sceptical, inquired how he killed his mother. Did the act not cause him to feel nausea? The Antelope explained to him that his mother had died from a disease and he tore off only her teeth because they were very precious. The teeth were precious because they would increase the life span. Buffalo was astonished again to hear that the teeth increased life. The Antelope told him that if you had 24 teeth, you would live only 24 years, and if you had 34 teeth then you would live 34 years. The Antelope had 32 teeth and his mother had 32 teeth also, so his life expectancy increased to 64 years. Upon hearing the Antelope, Buffalo was sad in his heart and was now thinking about a way to kill his mother for her teeth so he could also increase the days of his life. He didn't believe how the small animal like the Antelope could live longer than him.

Buffalo did not sleep well all the night; and during the day, he walked a little bit far in the hope to find his mother. Since Buffalo grew up, he gave up his life in the herd; confident of his strength to live alone. But the story of the teeth had grown on him to search for his parents. In his walk, he crossed a herd of Zebras who were quietly grazing on grass. Knowing the behaviour of the Buffalo; the Zebras avoided him completely. From afar, Buffalo was looking at the Zebras' bodies but did not get close to distinguish male and females. In the evening, whilst returning back home, he asked his friend, the Antelope, why the Zebras had black and white stripes, all of them males and females? The Antelope responded that Zebras were amazons, all of them were females. The Antelope explained to the Buffalo that all Zebras were females; therefore, they call them Amazons and their skins had stripes to attract the males. The Buffalo decided to conquer one of the amazons. The Antelope found his friend and companion to be a moron and did not want to give him exact answers or tell him the truth. It was true that Buffalos could be considered as a secondary animal. He was satisfied only with his surroundings, whereas the Antelope moved all the time to meet other animals and he discovered many things. He was making fun of Buffalo to answer him in this way; but Buffalo did not understand anything. The day Buffalo would discover Antelope's schemes would be the end of the friendship.

One day, Buffalo trotted himself far away from his preferred place. He had two things in his head; to find his mother to see whether he could tear off her teeth and to find some amazons because he wanted to conquer one amazon to cohabit together.

But where he passed, Monkeys were playing on the branch of the trees. They saw him and were very astonished to see the Buffalo walking around. Then the Monkeys asked him what he was doing in this place, distant from his habitat. He answered them that he was searching for the amazons, thinking that the Monkeys also knew this world about amazons created by his friend, the Antelope. They looked between themselves upon hearing this new word. While speaking to the Buffalo, the Monkeys were perched on the branches of the tree safely because of carefulness of life. Monkeys never came down on the ground, the Monkeys asked him again who amazons were? And Buffalo confirmed that it was the female animal that carries black and white stripes on her skin. The Monkeys told him that they would be able to help him find the amazons but not today, maybe tomorrow. The Buffalo was very satisfied and very happy while returning home. And in the evening, Buffalo told his friend, the Antelope, about his meeting with the Monkeys who promised to find one amazon for him. The Antelope, astonished, asked the Buffalo if the Monkeys had really promised him such things, knowing that this story of amazons was false. And the following day, very early, Antelope anticipated and went to find the Monkeys first and explained to them not to expose him to the Buffalo. Upon discovering his lie, Buffalo could kill him. Being good Monkeys, they agreed to protect the Antelope. When the Buffalo arrived, the Monkeys explained to him that amazons had immigrated because it was the dry season. The Monkeys planned a secret mission amongst them to know why Antelope was risking his life by handling Buffalo up to this point. And the Monkeys also explained to Buffalo that from time to time, Amazon could come to be refreshed at the back of the river and by chance he could meet them. But he had to be careful of the Crocodiles in the river. Buffalo assured them that he was not afraid of the Crocodile and no animal in the world would make him afraid. The Monkeys from the top of the trees made fun of the Buffalo's arrogance. Thus, the Buffalo started to position on the bank of the river while waiting for the arrival of the amazon. Buffalo had the habit of grazing at the bank of the river and looked at how water ran on the nest of the river.

One day, Buffalo saw a big lump surface on the river, full of people inside.

It was a boat which transported people towards the interior of the country in different villages. In this region of the world, people travel on boat coming from the big cities to go to villages to buy food less expensive than the urban areas. Of course, by making these purchases these people came to sell their goods in big cities by quoting it very expensive thus obtaining profit. Also, the transport in boats was adapted most favourably because the tickets were cheaper.

Then at that time of the season, the boat was full of people travelling to the villages. And Buffalo was there at the bank of the river looking at the boat.

People started to make an uproar to the Buffalo because of the way he was looking at them. Whilst returning home, he told the Antelope the discovery of the day. And asked the Antelope why people piled themselves in big boats and surfed the water? The Antelope answered him that the people were hungry and would seek food in the villages far away where food was less expensive. The Buffalo was astonished that people did not have food and had to travel long distances to nourish themselves. Whereas, he had all that he wanted to satisfy his hunger right around him. The Buffalo had pity on these people. And another day, when he was on the bank of the river, in the same place; he saw another boat full of people. By looking at them, the Buffalo raised his muzzle whilst grazing his grass. He was like a man sitting on a terrace, very relaxed having his breakfast.

By looking at these travellers, the Buffalo said to himself, "Poor people, it is terrible to make a journey to find something to eat; look at me," and he raised his muzzle, "I am always here and satisfied and well fed, breathing the fresh air instead of piling up in the boat."

While the travellers in the boat wondered, why the Buffalo looked at them in this manner. Of course, Buffalo was an ignorant animal who never saw a boat, really a stupid animal, they were all saying between themselves. Then the travellers made fun of the Buffalo and made an uproar by saying, "Look at the stupid Buffalo who does not even know that it is a boat moving in the water."

Then, among the travellers there was a teacher who attentively followed the scene and especially the behaviour of the Buffalo. All the travellers, including the teacher, said that

Buffalo was an idiot animal, really a stupid animal who did not understand what occurs. On his side, the Buffalo did not arrive to imagine, how a boat could float on water carrying a whole heap of people with him. The Buffalo thought in his manner and the travellers were also thinking in their manner. The Buffalo made fun of them showing them his muzzle that he was eating and a glance of mockery because it did not need to take a boat to seek food. Upright peacefully at the bank of the river and the only concern for him was that the rain was not coming quickly to refresh his body. At that time, it was the dry season.

In September, the traveller teacher had taken up the way of the school to discover his new pupils because it was the return of school. The image of the stupid Buffalo which looked at the boat remained in his memory. And while teaching, it happened that the students didn't understand and remained pensive by looking at the teacher. The teacher didn't like this habit of being looked at pensively, which made him remember the Buffalo. The teacher wanted that his students raised their arm when he asked a question and not look at him pensively. If one raised the arm and all of them had their eyes looking at him, the teacher shouted, "Please stop looking at me like the stupid Buffalo is looking at the boat." The pupils found this behaviour of the teacher very amusing and some of them started to imitate him, until the teacher had the nickname of 'Mister Stupid Buffalo' and this reached the mouths of all the students. It happened that one weekend one of the pupils was walking with his parents and met the teacher. The pupil told his parents that's our teacher 'Mister Stupid Buffalo'. The parents were very astonished to hear this nickname and asked their child to stop calling the teacher this name. Among the teachers of the school, 'Mister Stupid Buffalo' had become the star teacher of the school because the pupils told this nickname to their friends and parents. The teacher did not realise the popularity which this title brought to him. Being the teacher, they did not want to make fun of him in his presence, but used this nickname in slide. Before, the teacher was a single person and soon he got married to a beautiful woman and his partner came to stay with him. Whilst walking in the area where they lived, people were pointing a finger at her, that's the wife of 'Mister stupid Buffalo'. Because she was also the wife of a teacher, a position which deserves good respect in society, as a habit, some people were greeting her with courtesy but when she turned her back, people were making fun of her. Whilst going to the market, the salesman always gave her a small present. But she wondered of the excessive attention given to her by the salesman. Then one day, one of the salesmen had an awkwardness to greet her by saying, "Hello, madam Stupid Buffalo." She did not say anything because she wondered where the stupid name came from. While returning home, she told the name to her husband, but the husband was in confusion because he recognised pronouncing this word in his classroom with his students. But how a salesman had this idea? He calmed his wife and reminded her to forget it because people liked to amuse too much, especially the salesman, to attract the customers. And at school, in the classroom, he asked his pupils, what he was called, and all the pupils answered his true name Mister Peter. It was normal that students couldn't venture to call him his nickname.

One day, Mister Peter was late and his pupils were already in the classroom, sitting whilst waiting for the arrival of the teacher. As you know there were always trouble makers amongst the pupils, and one of them went to the front of the classroom and started to make comedy to amuse his colleagues. And in his comedy, he started to imitate Mister Peter in the way he shouted, "Don't look at me like the stupid Buffalo is looking at the boat." He put his hands in his pocket and started amusing his colleagues. The entire class were watching the way he was walking, and he went to the blackboard and wrote 'I am the Stupid Buffalo' while making a face. He turned his back from the main door, and at this moment, the teacher entered the classroom. All the class ceased laughing, but him, he didn't know that the teacher was in the classroom. And the teacher came to hold him from behind. While he turned, he was opposite to the teacher. His parents were summoned and the pupil was dismissed from the school. When the parents came to the school, they met the teacher's wife, and the woman recognised the salesman from the market.

While returning onto their premises, the woman and the teacher recognised that the husband had carried the nickname of 'Mister Stupid Buffalo'.

The Buffalo continued his excursions on the bank of the river. And one day, while returning, he noticed the Monkeys eating banana plantains, something he had never tasted. As usual, he asked to taste. He appreciated the taste of the plantains and later he passed the Monkeys each time after his walk to beg for plantains. And another day, like one says, "every day is not Sunday", the Monkeys didn't have any more plantains. The Buffalo was annoyed and shouted at the Monkeys, treating them like selfish animals. A male Giraffe who was passing in trimmings wanted to intervene to calm the Buffalo, but he had a blow of head in his bum which he would remember all his life. The Monkeys followed the scene from the top of the tree. The giraffe fell down and withdrew itself, whilst running he was swearing never again to intervene himself in the business of others. The Buffalo turned now towards the Monkeys and asked them again for plantains. But the Monkeys were very timorous and promised him to pass by again tomorrow.

According to the Buffalo, the world belonged to the rabbles and the strongest. For him, as he was strong; he nourished at the expense of the weak. In the event of refusal, you would get a good lesson and be obliged not to disobey the large master; the Buffalo rabble. The giraffe had a good lesson and would not approach the big master anymore. The Buffalo was now being nourished by the Antelope and Monkeys. The Buffalo was a villainous animal which wanted to dictate and force his colleagues and other animals to do what he wanted. It felt like he was the most daring and extremely strong. The evidence was that he had the energy to hold on the bank of the river being wary to the human being which surfaced on the limps according to him. he was sure that nobody would approach or ask him what he was doing on the bank of the river, whether man or animal.

The Monkeys and the Antelope were fed up of Buffalo and wanted to get rid of him.

The Monkeys explained the problem to the old Monkey, the veteran of the group and the most intelligent who had many life experiences. The old Monkey advised his fellow members that as the Buffalo was a greedy animal who liked to taste foods, it was better to prepare a food for him of poisonous mushrooms to easily get rid of him. By listening to that, all the Monkeys accepted this idea. As he was a greedy animal, he would ask to taste the mushrooms, then during the night he would fall sick and die, and you would be free and in peace. From there, there would be no more confrontation with such an animal. However, before putting the idea into action the Monkeys first had to find these poisonous mushrooms and invite the Buffalo. The Monkeys also thought to inform the Antelope about the blow they were plotting. When they asked the Antelope, he was totally in agreement with them. During this time, the Monkeys became very nice towards Buffalo by offering him all kinds of fruits. And also trying to chat with him for a long time thus creating a major friendship so that when a small Monkey climbed on the back of the Buffalo, he didn't react. The others shouted to the children to be wary about the Buffalo after his departure. Then the old Monkey, the veteran, brought the poisonous mushrooms. The Monkeys prepared the food with the fruits that the Buffalo knew for them to eat and the food of poison mushroom for the Buffalo. They were sure that the Buffalo, unaware of the mushroom, would ask to taste this. This time the Monkeys came down on the ground to welcome Buffalo by proposing the dish of mushrooms.

But Antelope excused himself from coming at this opportunity. The Antelope was a very intelligent and wise animal. He was avoiding to participate in such a party in case things turn bad. But the Antelope wished that while returning in the evening Buffalo would be sick under the effect of the poison.

Then the Buffalo went to the party to meet the Monkeys. Hardly arrived, he was attracted by the presence of an old Monkey who he had never seen before. The old Monkey was sat quietly in his place, moved away a little bit from them and looked at how things would unfold. All the Monkeys were sitting in a circle around each other, and each one with his dish on the side. Then a female Monkey brought a dish to the Buffalo of bananas plantains and poisonous mushrooms. But Buffalo noted that everyone had a dish except the old Monkey. The Monkeys welcomed Buffalo and also presented the old Monkey as the veteran of the group whom they owed much respect. The old Monkey was sitting under the shade of the tree. In this time of the heat, human beings or old animals liked to shelter under the shade of the tree to protect against the solar rays which were very prickly. And also, considering their old body, old people or old animals needed to take a little rest all the time. The old Monkey then took the word by wishing good appetite to everyone. Before starting to eat, Buffalo took his plate and came in front of the old Monkey and said that it was impolite to leave a veteran without food whilst everyone else was eating. Buffalo gave his plate to the old Monkey. Buffalo explained that in the old custom it was necessary to honour the oldest. The old Monkey must eat the first.

The old Monkey looked at the plate; he knew that they were the poisonous mushrooms that he himself brought. The old Monkey cherished his beard and looked at the sky, *What to do?* The big Buffalo was just upright in front of him, waiting for the old Monkey to eat the food in front of him. Surely the Buffalo did not know that the food was poisoned and the act which he made was only out of respect for the old Monkey. The Monkey already had sweat on his face. He did not know what to do at this time, knowing that the food was poisoned and told himself, "I am not going to die like an idiot, but what shall I do? Buffalo is just in front." And behind him, the large trunk of tree covered him, and in front was the Buffalo. Other Monkeys and the Chief of the group which were sitting behind Buffalo, understood that the veteran Monkey was in danger. The Chief of the group put himself behind Buffalo in an angle that his eyes could be in contact with the old Monkey.

He started to speak to him in sign language by making signs to the old Monkey not to eat this food. If the Buffalo discovered the trickery he would be inserted directly onto the old Monkey and he would kill him. The other Monkeys had their hands on their head because they saw already the misfortune of the poor old Monkey. In this similar situation, Monkeys react like human beings by putting their hands on their head as a sign of misfortune. The Chief of the group continued to make gestures to the old Monkey; his two eyes largely opened.

After this moment there was a large noise behind them, because a small Monkey made a bad jump and missed to catch a branch. The fall made an enormous noise that everybody turned over to see what occurred, and Buffalo also made an about turn. The old Monkey was relieved because at the moment the Buffalo turned away, he jumped with an incredible speed on the tree which was the nearest). And by seeing the old Monkey free, released by the influence of the Buffalo, all of them jumped on the tree and everyone ran away. The Buffalo did not understand anything, the old Monkey threw away his food and everyone fled. He looked all around and thought maybe the Monkeys saw the presence of a dangerous animal. He was now alone in the place without discovering any unspecified danger. In the final analysis, he decided to leave and ventured to his place, dissatisfied of the situation which had just occurred. But he thought already to ask the Monkeys for the explanation.

The night was quiet between Buffalo and Antelope. Each one spent the night in his corner as usual. In the morning Antelope woke up first, but Buffalo was still asleep. The Antelope thought that the Buffalo was under the effect of the poison. He did not know what happened yesterday with the Monkeys. Then he took a sheet and started to agitate in front of the Buffalo's eyes, to know if Buffalo was dead. Precisely, Buffalo howled when he saw a sheet in front of his face! And the Antelope made an excuse in front of him, and answered that he drove out a fly which disturbed him. The Antelope was now in doubt; this jerk, the Buffalo, did not eat the poison! It was necessary to go and see the animals.

This morning, the Buffalo went straight to the banks of the river without passing a single place. He was thirsty to find a female partner. His instinct was right, and he found an amazon drinking water. For him, all the Zebras were amazons, as his friend, the Antelope, had explained to him. Whereas that was a male Zebra drinking water at the bank of the river. The Buffalo approached him politely because he knew Zebras were afraid of him. Buffalo spoke to him with fine words and finally asked him whether he could help him. The male retorted to Buffalo that he was not an amazon, but if he wants assistance, he could help him.

Buffalo burst out laughing by saying, "It is good if you prefer to be called Zebra." Buffalo accepted and was thinking that the Zebra refused the name because he had the conscience of a prostitute.

The Zebra was surprised by the friendship which Buffalo suggested to him. He thought that it was not really his best day because the Lions attacked him and here, during the day, the Buffalo called him amazon.

Buffalo requested the Zebra to accompany him to see the Monkeys, because he knew that he could have something to eat and to offer his new companion.

During the journey he continued to cheer up the Zebra by telling him that he was a good animal and that he needed to find friends like him. The Zebra didn't answer, but thought about the remarks of the Buffalo when they arrived at the Monkeys' place and the two companions found the Antelope discussing with the Monkeys about the mishap that happened yesterday. The presence of Buffalo and Zebra stopped the conversation between Antelope and the Monkeys. Buffalo arrived, smiling, and revealed to Antelope that he found his beloved amazon. But the Zebra counteracted by forcefully saying that he was not a female but a male. The Buffalo looked at the Antelope so that he could explain the enigma. The Buffalo asked the Antelope, "But you told me, that all Zebras are born female but now this one declares to be male!"

The Monkeys from the top of the tree burst out laughing, then Buffalo understood the trickery of the Antelope. Buffalo, raging mad, desired to crush the Antelope with one blow. For the Raffish that he was, there was no pity for the bastard like Antelope. Buffalo rubbed his hoofs as a sign of anger to attack the Antelope. The Antelope understood the danger, and thought of how to get rid of the mastodon.

Then, at a stretch, he shouted, "Buffalo, you cannot do anything against me because I know your secret. Move back now and I will prove to everyone present here how I will thrash you".

The Buffalo was surprised by the language of the Antelope and stopped in a dash. It was the first time that Antelope spoke to him with authority. The Antelope walked to and fro with great steps. He asked the Zebra to move forward and give space because he was going to hurt Buffalo. And Antelope looked at the Buffalo and said, "Do you know how the fly, a small insect, killed the Elephant? That's what will happen to you now."

The Monkeys from the top of the trees, looked at the scene. The Chief of the group explained that he saw the Antelope had been consulting with witchcraft.

And the others said, "I can't see how he can fight with Buffalo, even if consulting witchcraft."

And the other Monkey also concluded, "I don't see what he's going to use against the fight with Buffalo, his small feet or his teeth, he even does not have a horn. Oh, my ancestors, help him. I don't want to be a witness of this scene."

But Monkey still looked at the scene. The female Monkey called the Chief of the group to give him a mango fruit but he refused, saying that he can't flunk such a thing that only comes into your life once.

The Zebra, on his side, also deplored by saying, really, it's not his best day.

Incredible, but true, Antelope wanted to fight Buffalo. Then the Antelope requested that Buffalo moved in front a little because the fight was going to start. Buffalo started to stammer thinking about what the Antelope wanted to do. The Antelope then requested Buffalo to countdown and all of them were wondering what would happen next. When Buffalo started to count, five, four, three, the Antelope looked behind him, the way was mostly empty.

He shouted to Buffalo, "Big fatty animal, you are only an idiot'" and ran away. The Antelope had a head start and had incredible speed. The Buffalo had not finished counting when the Antelope had already disappeared. Then Buffalo got angry and started to knock everything in front of him. Monkeys shouted; what an exploit!

Seeing the anger of Buffalo, the Monkeys also began to run away, in the same way Zebra also disappeared into the horizon. This was how the friendship between Buffalo and Antelope ended. Buffalo decided that this jerk handled him as blind animal but the day I would catch him, he would regret being born!

Chapter 13

'History of the Brown Dog'

The Dog: Beloved Animal

The Dog is a pet most beloved among animals because he behaves as a good guard. He is flexible to his master, and he always seeks to defend the interest of his owner. Not only is he a protective animal but he also works to help his master.

During the night Dog takes care, and protects the master and his family against the strange intrusion from outside; whether it's human beings or animals and even evil spirits which grinds during the night. The advantage of the Dog is that he barks to communicate to the others, especially to his master. This barking frightens the intruder and he runs away. During the night he acts like a watchman whom the master uses free for his security. The man also uses the Dog in his work, especially the hunters. In killing an animal, a Dog takes care to find the game and bring him to the master.

The natives loved the Dogs, especially for their protection against the evil spirits which grinded in the night. In this region, far away from the modern civilisation, the man preferred the Dog as compared to other animals; even the cats did not get that much admiration. The problem with the cat was that he cooperated with the Leopard and he praised this cooperation because he finds food and protection. The cat liked to trot during the night, but the Dog and the man had a rest during this time. During the night the cat did his business, which the natives and villagers found odd. The cat was a spy, acting in the service of the Leopard. He located the place where sheep were sleeping during the day and at night he communicated with the Leopard, then later, they shared the loot. It was in this context that the cat made fun of the Dog when he ate the bones thrown by man. When he himself nourishes on fresh meat which he shared with his friend, the Leopard. Among the pets, the Dog was the animal which did much work by helping the man in his daily occupation, but also the animal was boldly nourished by the man. The cat and other animals spent their day by dowsing. How to explain this behaviour of man towards his friend, the Dog, who he did not take care of properly.

The Dog was an animal which lived in good relationship with man and his accomplice animals. The Brown Dog, named Paul, was living with his owner and other animals like the cat, sheep and the Goat. In the morning the owner of the sheep, the Shephard, brought the sheep to the pastorage to graze the grass and in the afternoon, he brought them back to the plot. Then the Brown Dog was very astonished to see the animals chewing something under their teeth at the time they were relaxed when there was nothing to eat in front of them. The Brown Dog was unaware that the sheep had ruminants and that they could keep food in their pockets and bring it in their mouth at any moment.

One day, whilst going to hunt with his master, the Brown Dog withdrew from him to converse with the Monkeys. He explained to the Monkeys how always the sheep were chewing something under their teeth, whereas there was nothing under them. The Monkeys were also unaware of the system of ruminants and wanted at any price to see the thing, as they were incredibly curious. The following day, the two Monkey friends of the Brown Dog came into the plot where the Brown Dog was living. The first thing which attracted them was the presence of the Goat who had a cord tied on his neck, and he was up the tree, is this slavery? The Brown Dog answered them that he was a very destitute animal.

Several times he ran away once he had freedom; so, it's better he is fastened so he did not escape. The Goat far away noted how the Monkeys looked at him. The Goat had never seen the Monkeys on their plot and thought that they were robbers who planned with the Dog. For the Goat, the Brown Dog was an animal who easily let himself get corrupt. At this moment the group of Monkeys and Dog started to approach the Goat. The Goat said to himself in his heart that the robbers were coming to corrupt him as well. The Monkeys had pity on the Goat who was being treated like a slave and they wanted to help him. Their intention was to explain to the Goat how to escape against this atrocity. But the Brown Dog was not happy with the intention of the Monkeys and he reminded them that they were here to find out what the sheep chewed all the time under his teeth. But one of the Monkeys, by seeing the Goat chewing, declared openly that they moved for nothing because the Goat was chewing cashew nut to strengthen his teeth.

The Brown Dog shouted, "But where does he find these cashew nuts when he does not move?"

The other Monkey explained that the Shephard brought it with the grass. The Brown Dog did not believe the assertion of the Monkeys. It was necessary to ask himself the Goat, this one confirmed that they were not robbers but rather insane animals. Since when does the Goat eat walnuts? The Goat did not understand anything about the walnut. To satisfy them, the Goat told them that he kept his walnuts in his pocket which is in his belly. The others, astonished by his assertion, burst out laughing to make fun of the Goat, "How can you have a pocket in your belly?"

At this moment, the owner appeared and noted that there were foreign animals on the plot. He wanted to chase them away but one of the Monkeys explained to the owner that they were friends and came to help the Goat to shave his beard. It was true that the beard of the Goat was falling from his chin like a bishop.

The owner contemplated the Goat's beard and said, "It's true, his beard deserves a shave."

When the owner disappeared, the Goat was astonished, wondering what the Dog and the Monkey wanted exactly. Then the Goat promised the tree animals to pass tomorrow because he would keep some walnuts for them. Tomorrow he would keep the grass to show them then they would understand. And he shouted at the Monkeys, telling them that no one could touch his beard. But the Brown Dog asked the Monkeys not to return to their plot because he does not want to compromise his friendship with the master, the owner. The Monkeys advised the Goat to escape because that was not life, to be always attached to a rope. The Brown Dog started to push the Monkeys to go far away. Now that the Goat promised them walnuts, the Monkeys started to plan their return during the night to release the Goat.

The Brown Dog was a very obedient animal who liked to protect the interest of his master. On the other hand, the big enemy of the Brown Dog was the Crocodile. The Brown Dog revealed Monkeys' plan to the owner and their plans to release the Goat failed and they did not come out anymore.

Once the Crocodile lived with the family. In the time of drought during the dry season, he missed food and especially, because his female was pregnant. It was necessary that she was nourished well to develop the eggs which she carried in her belly. That's why the male Crocodile decided to leave water to seek game in the Savannah. He went far from the river and after a long and toiling day, he caught a young Antelope. It was really difficult for him to catch this animal because it was necessary to hide in the grass and to gently approach the herd of Antelopes who were also very vigilant. A little rustle and the animals could flee because they were the prey of predators. But the Crocodile had an advantage in this situation because he moved low on his belly, contrary to other animals. This advantage of crawling by ground, enabled him to catch an unhappy young Antelope. Then the Crocodile, very tired, returned to the river with his burden on his back. On his way, he crossed his friend, the Brown Dog. At that time, the two animals were very friendly. As he was too tired, he asked his friend, the Brown Dog, if he could help him.

He said to the Brown Dog, "As you run quickly, please, can you take this young Antelope and deliver it to my wife who is pregnant. Surely, she would be dying of hunger. I have left her since this morning without food. As soon as you arrive at the bank of the river, just throw the stones three times in the water, and she would come out."

The Brown Dog agreed to help his friend, the Crocodile, and he took the game and started to run towards the river. But in the course of the journey, he stopped and looked at the game and he was hungry as well. Now he did not run anymore but started walking with small steps whilst thinking about the game. He met an old Dog on his way who enquired where he was going with the game. The Brown Dog answered that the game belonged to the Crocodile and his family. And the old Dog replied that he was very generous to help the Crocodile, an animal that lives in the water. The Brown Dog carried on his way, ignoring the advice of the old Dog, but the hunger corroded his belly. *He, who only eats bones from the master, and here, in front of him is fresh meat, what to do?*

He carried on his way and there he met a group of Dogs who asked him the same questions. He explained to them the origin and the destination of the game.

"You are not in security whilst transporting the game because you can be attacked by gangsters," the group of Dogs advised him to share the game instead of risking his life. But the Brown Dog refused because there were four Dogs and to share with them would not satisfy his hunger. He indicated to the group of Dogs that he did not agree with them, and if they used force, he would denounce them to the Crocodile. The group of Dogs were afraid and let him go. And after some hundred meters of walking, he met his friend Dog, who was alone. The Brown Dog knew that his friend would have asked about the game and he took the lead by announcing that he was going quickly to give Crocodile his game. But his friend told him to be calm for a minute and took him to a quiet corner where there was some shade. The friend told him that for three days he had been nearly dying of hunger. The Brown Dog shouted to his ancestors that it was a trap; this game would not arrive to its destination. The friend advised him to share the game and forget the Crocodile because the Crocodile lived in water and we Dogs on the ground. There was nothing to be afraid of and the Crocodile would never come to recover his game. By listening to these pretty words from his friend, the Brown Dog accepted the offer and said to himself, "Why not eat this game when I am hungry and my friend is hungry. I don't care about this crazy Crocodile. Let us eat this game." So, Brown Dog accepted because it was also his wish. That evening was a festival for the two friends, as they were accustomed to eating the remains of bones.

The male Crocodile, whilst arriving at the river, found his wife starving without food since the morning, and he discovered the trick of the Dog. The Crocodile started shouting "Brown Dog, you did that to me. It is true you live on the ground and I live in the water, but the day I will see you in the water or at the bank of the river I will not miss my revenge." That was why the Brown Dog became the number one enemy of the Crocodile.

Since old times, the natives suffered attacks repeatedly by Crocodiles at the time they crossed the river. Often the natives used dugouts to cross the river for the exchange of food. If they were only humans, they passed the river quietly but if the Dog was in the dugout, the Crocodile did not hesitate to attack them. And often the Crocodile would confuse even sheep or Goats in the dugouts and attack them.

Those who suffered more and often lost their lives were townsman who came to supply the goods to the native people. Especially smoke fish which they bought cheap and sold expensively. Most of the townsman could not swim and if it was not the Crocodile that killed them, they perished by drowning. For the natives, things were easy and they were called children of the water, because they were born with water and grew with water. The Crocodile did not attack on the border of the river, but rather in the middle where the river is deep. The townsmen who came to supply themselves to the natives were obliged to adapt the quality of this life. The natives sometimes advised their friends never to venture or swim in the river. If there were Crocodiles which attacked in the middle of the river because of the presence of the Dog, it was noted that they only attacked the foreigners. Incredible, but true; these Crocodiles never attacked the natives or their children, who ventured to swim in the river.

While seeking to discover the truth, the natives themselves said they were fetish Crocodiles used by the fisherman to trap much fish to satisfy the demand of the townsman. Basically, the native fisherman had to sacrifice a human being to receive the food output. Then, by fear of reprisal, the fisherman sent the Crocodile to attack the foreigners. It was similar with the hunters, who advised people not to eat a fruit or other things from unknown field. It was necessary to respect the others' food; in the event of disobedience, the curse could catch you. The hunters had a complicity with the drill, like fisherman had with the river. We must know that fishermen, called fisher of WAGEMIA, could remain in the water one hour and even take their breakfast in water such as the cassava cooked with peanuts; food which could not dissolve in water.

The Dog was a good companion to the man. Even though human being misused him, he remained the most appreciated animal beloved by man. There was an example of a man who wanted to get rid of a Dog because he was fed up of him. He took the Dog and brought him to a river to drown him. Unfortunately, at the place where he wanted to drown his Dog, water was very deep. By pushing his Dog, he was attacked by the current of the water and started to drown himself. He shouted for help but nobody was coming to his help. He wanted to kill the Dog without anyone seeing him. Seeing his master in anguish, the same Dog helped his master to shore. The man started to vomit water and looked at his Dog and thanked him for saving his life. But when they arrived in the village, the man gave up his Dog and went to live faraway to prevent the Dog from following him. This history brought the natives to make the reflection 'the thanks without affection which one gave to the Dog', which means thanks which does not come from the heart, but simply to make fun of the person or animal concerned.

The Brown Dog did not want to come into contact again with the Monkeys because they planned to give the Goat bad advice so that he could leave his master. In the case that the master discovered the trick, it was him who would have problems. The Brown Dog was a pet and he preferred to have the master to look after him. He was really sad to see a Dog which did not have a master; he would be roaming everywhere and had difficulty finding the food. The life of hunting rats in the drill was not compatible to the life of a Dog. It was true also for a man who became a tramp; a man without shelter, this man was in the same situation like the Dog without his master. The Brown Dog knew this situation, as he had seen some Dogs wandering around the village. The Brown Dog did not want to end up in this situation and it is for this reason that he ended up being faithful to his master. Even on seeing the Goat grazing grass he was very satisfied or seeing the cat relaxed, all these did not disturb him and he remained faithful to his master. The Brown Dog thought that his sorrow was enough for him and he was well in this situation because each night he had bones to crush. Each evening, after a hard day, he was sitting always under the tree in the same place.

The master of the Brown Dog had a friend who visited him each evening. It was the practice of the natives after a hard day; at sunset, he would bring around palm wine and they would exchange ideas. Then, by seeing the Brown Dog sat in the corner alone, he advised his friend to find a female Dog to share his life. In this case, the Brown Dog would have someone to have fun and spend the evening with. The master thought that the idea was good and began to seek a female for the Brown Dog. The day the master brought a bitch in the compound, you should have seen how happy Brown Dog was. He laughed at everyone and moved his tail as a sign of thanks to the master because it was an act the Brown Dog had not expected. After many months of normal life, the bitch conceived.

For the master, this was normal, there was no objection that the female was pregnant, until the female gave birth to twelve puppies! The master himself did not come and see the new-born pups. The Brown Dog was doing everything himself to nourish his female and the small pups. After one month the pups grew and their presence started to get noticed in the compound. Another day, as usual, the master, with the Brown Dog, returned home from hunting. And while entering the compound, the puppies backed up everywhere, running and having fun as all children do.

Then the master asked, "where have all these Dogs come from?"

The brown Dog answered with arrogance that they were his puppies. The master was not happy to see all these puppies populating his compound. The wife of the master also, on her side, was expecting the return of her husband to complain about the presence of all the puppies in the compound. The next morning, the master invited the Brown Dog to ask him how he could nourish twelve small puppies plus the two parents, totalling fourteen Dogs! The master made an excuse to the Brown Dog that he could not keep all the population of the Dogs in his compound. So, he must leave the place. The problem with the natives was that they could not castrate animals. The master was expecting brown Dog to produce at least two puppies, but not more than ten.

The following day, the master and his wife decided to repudiate Brown Dog with his partner and their small pups. *The man is born selfish*, thought the Brown Dog, *whereas the natives in their families live in a widened family but when it's about an animal, things become impossible.* The Brown Dog was obliged to leave the house of his master and his family for an unknown place.

The Monkeys, on seeing their friend given up by his master, went to inform the Goat, the guard of the animals. The Goat, father of all animals, lodged the Brown Dog with his family. Fortunately, one priest agreed to take Brown Dog with his family, but with a condition to castrate the family Dog. The Brown Dog accepted this with pleasure. The monastery needed the Dogs to keep the fields and to supervise harvest against intruders. The priest was glad to raise the small pups because after growing they would take over their father to watch the fields.

As the priest had a Dog before, he had kept canned food for Dogs. And that evening, he brought the tin to Mr Brown's family. But Brown Dog was surprised to see the priest opening the tin because he never saw a tin of food for animals. And even more surprising, there was a picture of Dog on the tin. The Brown Dog refused to eat the meat from the tin and recommended his family not to touch this abominable food! The priest was also surprised by the refusal of Mr Brown for not eating the tinned meat. Then the priest explained to Mr Brown that the food is for Dogs and it came from Europe. Therefore, there was a picture of a Dog on it. Brown Dog was thinking that the meat inside the tin was flesh of a Dog. The brown Dog didn't believe this about the tin by saying how was it the Dogs in Europe had tins of meat whereas, for them, they were satisfied by crumbs of bones or catching rats in the drill.

The following day, the Goat passed the monastery to see how Brown Dog and his family behaved. The Goat enquired of Mr brown how his new house was going and Brown Dog confirmed that he could not sleep well. The Goat was astonished to hear that, as the place was more immense than his old master's house and the priests were good people. Brown Dog assured him that it was not about the accommodation but they had to eat the meat contained in the tin, "Can you realise that Dogs were starving here and other Dogs had tinned food?"

The Goat felt bad by hearing the declaration of Brown Dog. But what could they do; the life was made like this. Brown Dog still did not understand how other Dogs like those who live in Europe could have tinned food! At this moment, the priest also arrived and Goat explained to him the concerns of Brown Dog. Both explained to Brown Dog that Europe was more developed than Africa and the situation of Dogs which live there was different to those like him who live in Africa.

Then Mr Brown asked another question, "Why don't people copy Europeans so we can be a developed country?" Brown Dog gave them the example of a shoemaker who lived in a corner, "if I want to be a shoemaker like him, I must copy his skill and practice with him to learn how to make a shoe. Why don't Africans copy European people, then Dogs would also have tinned food in Africa? But people had preferred to live in misery by looking at Europe! Then Brown Dog asked the priest if he wanted to discover Europe?"

The priest told him that there were many people who required asylum. Then Brown Dog, surprised, asked if he could also seek asylum. But the priest and the Goat didn't want to sadden Brown Dog by saying that asylum was only for human beings. And the priest explained to the Brown Dog that there were people who had political problems, or their life was in danger and they would require asylum in Europe. The Brown Dog told the priest that he would seek asylum and would raise the issue of tshibele-bele because it was believed that the tin the priest gave to them was flesh of a Dog. The Goat shouted to his ancestors to help him; by raising the question, what does Brown Dog finally want! The priest did not know what was meant by tshibele-bele and he requested the explanation from the Goat. The Goat explained to the priest and the Brown Dog that the problem of tshibele-bele was the practice that the natives made at the time of festivals or weddings. They killed the Dog and cooked the meat for the bride and groom.

This meat was blessed by the two families and to wish a happy offspring for the couple. But the young people revolted against this practice because the Dog was considered as a friend of the family, even as a pet. And at the time of an event, to kill this friend, it looked like one was killing a close relative. The new generation said no to this insane practice. The new generation had refused to adhere to this illogical practice. The priest was surprised by the intelligence of the Brown Dog and promised to bring him to Europe so that he was well satisfied with the tin.

The idea of brown Dog was not bad. One of Africa's comedians made this reflection.

One day, God would see people suffering too much, he would come on earth and tell the people he wanted to bless all the people to have a better life. To have a blessing, you need to ask one thing that God would give you with the condition that your neighbour would have double.

Then God asked the white man, “What do you want, son?” White man said he wanted 5,000,000 cows. Then God said, “I would give you 5,000,000 cows but your neighbour would get 10,000,000.” White man said that it’s fine!

Then God asked the Asian man, “What do you want, my son?” The Asian man said he wants 10,000,000 money. Then God said, “I would give you but your neighbour would get 20,000000.” Asian man said that it’s okay.

Now God came to the African man, “What do you want, my son?” The African man started to think, *If I ask God for 10,000,000 cows, my neighbour will get 20,000,000*. Then the African man told God to wait a bit. After reflection, the African man told his wife, “Really if I ask for 10,000,000 cows, this arrogant neighbour would receive 20,000,000.” Finally, the African man said to God, “I want to stay the way I am; this means poor.” The new generation of leaders and, especially, African people think that poverty in Africa is coming from ourselves. The future will tell us!

Chapter 14
'Back Home'

In the village Virunga, where the name of Paul Virunga came from; the son of the Chief was likely to grant a subvention from the government, which had allowed him to travel towards Europe. The subvention was not at the range of everyone. But the son of the Chief was likely to obtain it, considering the actions of his father for the protection of animals. The Chief of the village Virunga and his notables had accepted to set up a national park very close to the village to protect animals. Then as a reward to help the Chief, the government of the country had granted a subvention to his son to go to Europe and continue his university study. He was a very intelligent boy who had made his primary and secondary school from the mission of catholic.

Today, the indigenous man felt guilty in his ignorance. When he saw the aeroplane flying in the sky; they asked themselves that it was a man who made the machine. But why were they isolated of the wellbeing of this machine! Not only isolated on the social progress also they didn't live like other people. Where it came from, this ignorance, asked the indigenous man. It was, thus, currently all good parents amongst the natives or indigenous, even the townsman, wished that their children received full education. That meant they needed to go to school. They did not want their history to be repeated in the lives of their children.

That means the ignorance missed instruction such as to be illiterate must be abolished in the life of their children. Because they understood that missed instruction and education constructed the intellectual development of the human being. From this point of view, it could be said that the future belonged to everyone, including the animals. If the indigenous man developed on the level of the townsman, there would be a progress for the protection of animals.

The killing of animals would be decreased as well. At the moment, the townsman was satisfied by toast bread produced by the baker for his breakfast, but the indigenous billed the man for his breakfast.

Until now the indigenous man was devoid of the humanity's progress. The natives had pity on themselves when they moved to the great urban areas.

They discovered another world where everything was written, the buses had numbers. Most of the illiterate did not arrive to control themselves. They had to get information from other people, sometimes very mistrustful, refusing to help them. A native was always recognisable by the way he was wearing clothes or by the way he was talking.

If the indigenous changed his mentality by eating the flesh of animals, some diseases from animals could be avoided. The indigenous or native men must be helped. The disease like Ebola, which scientists confirm to have had come from the flesh of animals, is a significant example. And there were always risks, that the diseases contracted by the indigenous or natives could be spread to the countries known as developed. The native or indigenous, the contractor of the disease, is always in contact with the townsman, then one likes to travel and is in contact with other people then the disease is propagated. If the modern man is aware by helping his counterpart, he would treat the indigenous man with the penicillin; this would mean the protection of all the world against certain diseases. And the indigenous arrived to a nourished clean product from the field.

After this analysis of the indigenous man, let us see the history of Seraph now, son of the Chief, descended from this indigenous world, where he had grown and had a chance to study in Europe. Virungu Village, where Seraph came from was a village located at the fine bottom of the Equatorial forest. And in this part of the world, there were only two seasons, rainy season and the cig season.

As you read in our previous paragraph, the indigenous and villagers liked the rain season. It was the season where the sheets of trees were green with the appearance of the multitude of insects attracted by the green trees. In Europe, where Seraph was doing his studies of Medicine, he met a European friend called Richard. Indeed, Richard was a botanist and he was doing research on the various types of insects. Seraph told him about the wealth of the insects and the vegetation of the equatorial forest. Then Richard, attracted by the wonders of the equatorial forest, decided to visit the area. While arriving at the village Virungu, the Chief, who was the father of Seraph, and his notables, accommodated Richard with enthusiasm.

All the village was happy to receive the child of the village who returned back with his European friend. The Chief, seeing his son coming back with a European, thought there would be progress in the village. Perhaps the European was a doctor in medicine or a public engineer, the village would be happy and it was him who would have all the honours. The young people and children in the village gathered, attracted by the presence of Richard. Every morning they waited to see their visitor and what he would do. Richard and Seraph slept in the same hut, especially arranged for them. One bedroom with two beds and a living room at the entry. Richard had a small night table where he was reading his booklet with a storm lantern. But during the day, Richard spends time in an open hut made with straw because of the heat. It was his workplace. After having a trot in the drill with two or three fluids, he came back writing his notes under his hut of straw and also to nibble some biscuits or a chocolate bar which he bought from Europe. Seraph had explained to his father and the nobles that they came to make some research with his friend, the white man, without specifying which type of research. The Chief and his nobles did not know which type of research his son and the white man wanted to make.

But as the days pass, they noted that the white man caught all kinds of Butterflies and Caterpillars, which he studied in his hut with a magnifying glass. Then the village started to wonder, what the white man would do with the insects that he caught. They were not into insects as they found them very harmful and gave them no importance, except for the Caterpillars which they eat. Then at the time that they see a white man leave his grounds and to come just to catch insects, they found this unbelievable. The children liked to follow Richard and sometimes they caught the Butterflies for Richard. Richard found it very amusing and at the end, he gave them chocolate and biscuits.

Around midday the weather was very hot. Richard returned to his hut to drink some water and nibble some bars of chocolate. And the practice amused the villagers by saying how a man could get all the nourishment from a bar of sweet. For them, sweets were for children and not an adult to eat for his lunch and they made fun of the white man who didn't want to eat a good meal with a bowl of cassava. From time to time, after having a food lunch, they were held a little bit further to contemplate Richard nibbling a bar of chocolate. For knowing why the white man nourished himself with chocolate, they sent children to ask questions to Richard. And Richard would also be making fun to the children by telling them that too much vitamins in chocolate and he didn't want to get fat.

On the other hand, the news was propagated in the village and its surroundings that the son of the Chief and his friend the European man came back home to catch insects. Whereas everyone expected to see Seraph returned to the village like a doctor or an engineer. The villagers started to make fun of the Chief. Then they would say among themselves, how the child of the village could leave his native land to go to study the insects in Europe? Some of them started to say that their boy was bewitched, as the Chief didn't want to give the chance to other children and look what his own son brought back for us…they study of insects. And these gossips reached the ears of the Chief, who convened a meeting with his nobles to find a solution. The nobles suggested driving the European out of the village because it was really a shame. But two nobles refused because it would give a bad image of the village. But a wizard who was amongst them advanced the idea to bewitch the European to leave the village in peace because he is an altruist who gives sweets to our children.

On the birthday of the Chief everyone thought to offer a gift to him. The villages had this habit because the gift that they gave to the Chief was a sign of allegiance. In the event of a problem in the future, the Chief could always help whilst thinking of the gift during his birthday. Then one hunter caught a large Tortoise who was really old and gave him to the Chief for his birthday, because the Tortoise was an animal which the Chief liked to eat because of his wisdom and life time. It was a man who would cook the animal and before cooking, there would be a magic incantation by the wizard for the wisdom and the long life to be transferred to the Chief. As usual, the news propagated in the village that the Chief had a nice gift for his birthday. Also, the children brought the news to Richard and the European man. Richard, the European, found the act abominable, as one shouldn't kill an animal for pleasure of somebody. He decided to go and see the Chief and ask him to release the animal. Mr Richard suggested to the Chief and his nobles that he would order a birthday cake from his embassy for the birthday of the Chief. Everyone made fun of the European and burst into laughter by saying now the white man wants to make us eat his sweets. The news was propagated in the village that the European wanted to offer sweets to the Chief for his birthday. Richard insisted and asked the Chief not to kill the Tortoise. The Chief, very impatiently, told Richard that he would think about it, but all the nobles backed up against Richard's ideas by saying that the white man deceived his son and now he wanted to force us to embrace his culture by eating all the sweets. And they insisted to all the wizards of the village to do something so that the European leaves the village as soon as possible.

The following day, the children came as usual to chatter with Richard. Then the young son of the Chief told Richard that he had nourished the Tortoise which was locked up in a small room. Richard asked him whether he was also friendly towards animals. He said, "Yes, of course," and Richard informed him that he was sad because the Tortoise would be killed one day. He asked the young son of the Chief if he could help him. Richard took the boy by the hand, to move away from his comrades, then he required the child to release the Tortoise at the time he would feed him and preferably during the night. The child accepted but on condition of increasing the menu of chocolates. The Tortoise was hidden in the background of the house of the Chief. The Chief's son and his cousin organised a plan to save the Tortoise. And the plan worked wonderfully. During the night when everyone was asleep, they opened the door and let the Tortoise escape in nature. The Tortoise thanked the kids and wondered why they had done that. The following day, they informed Richard and asked him to keep the secret, not a word to another person; even to Seraph. Thus, the life continued, even the Chief and his nobles did not suspect the disappearance of the Tortoise. They believed that the animal was always there in the room.

And many times, they threw green shrubs and fruit to nourish him. In the room where they left the Tortoise, the ground was covered with lots of mixed stones because they knew that the Tortoise could dig the ground and be free. It was this way that the Tortoise usually would escape from his prison.

This evening, whilst going to his bedroom, Richard noticed a mosquito was flying around the room. He took his book notes to mend with his stem paper, now many mosquitoes were flying around the room. At one moment, all the mosquitoes disappeared, there were no mosquitoes around and he decided to sleep. But in the middle of the night, the room was full up of mosquitoes. The mosquitoes started to bite him everywhere, sometimes on his leg. When he focused on his leg, they started to bite him on his back. Richard, did not sleep well. But when he looked, Seraph was sleeping like a baby; no mosquitoes were biting him. In the morning, Richard asked Seraph if he noticed the presence of mosquitoes during the night. But Seraph answered that he had to stop dreaming because there were no mosquitoes. Then he showed him the bites of mosquitoes on his skin. But Seraph did not want to believe that the bites were from a mosquito, they may be from other insects during the day. The day passed quietly and Richard did not feel any bites on his body when he was catching Butterflies in the bush.

As soon as the night fell and after having switched on his lamp, one mosquito whistled into the room and drew the attention of Richard. At this moment, Seraph was laying on his bed reading a book without being concerned about anything. Few moments later, Seraph started to snore and sleep deeply. Then the mosquito came back again, and started to displaying acrobatics in the air under the distressful look of Richard. The mosquito turned to do acrobatics in the form of the number eight. Richard looked at the mosquito and called him a super mosquito because of the acrobatics which he made. Richard did not sleep well because a cloud of mosquitoes prevented him from sleeping. They bit him everywhere; it was a nightmare for Richard. When he went to sleep, he heard the whistle of mosquitoes on the top of his head and at the same time, one bit him on the leg. He could not control himself. He was awake and tried to drive out the mosquitoes. When he looked at Seraph, he was asleep quietly without being disturbed by the mosquitoes. As it was very hot during the night, Richard slept only with his underpants. This night again Richard did not sleep well, having nightmares because of the mosquitoes which bit him everywhere. When he heard whistles on the front of his head, his attention focused on the place where it was coming from. But it was on the opposite direction that the mosquitos bit. At the time when he switched on the lamp, his companion was asleep like a baby. He wondered whether these mosquitoes knew he was a foreigner. In the morning, Richard went to see Mr Maurice, the postman who came to collect letters from the village to post in town.

Mr Maurice had a scooter and wore glasses. Mr Maurice always had a smile on his lips and liked to have fun with small children.

After having collected his letters and small parcels, Mr Maurice did acrobatics with his scooter; he did acrobatics in the form of two circles as the number eight, exactly like the super mosquito during the night. Richard was wondering if there was a connection between the two phenomena! In this letter he had sent to his friend who works in the embassy, he requested insecticides because he was very annoyed by the presence of the insects.

The days passed, then the birthday of the Chief arrived. The notable sent the cook, the man who must cook the Tortoise to kill the animal in front of the Chief. Because this animal had to be cooked by a man and all the women and children were completely isolated. The notables advised the man to make a nice soup because the animal must have increased his weight, considering how well he was nourished. The door of the room where the Tortoise was placed was well locked. The cook entered and sought everywhere but the Tortoise was not there. Only foliage and fruit which one threw to nourish the animal remained. The man left while running and shouted that the Tortoise had disappeared. The Chief and the notables, astonished, ran into the room to check properly; maybe the Tortoise had made a hole, but nothing of that sort. One notable laid hands on his head as if a misfortune had arrived and shouted that the magic of the white man had made the Tortoise disappear. He didn’t want us to kill the Tortoise. The Chief called everyone who lived in the house if they saw the Tortoise but nobody confirmed to have seen the animal. The Chief and the notables asked themselves the question, *how could this animal escape?* Only the white man could do this thing. He should be a very strong wizard.

The Tortoise, after being set free, convened an assembly of the animals and explained to them this mishap. That Tortoise was an old one, who had many life experiences. His goal was to explain to his contemporary why man wants always to eat the flesh of the animals. To hear that, the Monkeys first admitted their incapacity against man's massacre and that they were the victims of men. The natives and villagers had their breakfast in the morning with meat of Monkeys boiled in salted water with cassava; they liked this menu. The same as a townsman ate bread in the morning with his coffee or cup of tea. Also, wild boars, Antelopes, Rhinos and Zebras confirmed these allegations that they were also victim of man's massacre. Only the Chimpanzees backed up, remaining mouths closed without saying a word.

The Tortoise inquired of the Chimpanzees, "what is the meaning of this silence?"

One of the Chimpanzees answered that they were not concerned about the massacre of the man. They said that maybe Monkeys were victims because they reproduced like pigs. Hearing this, a quarrel erupted between the Chimpanzees and the Monkeys. But the mastodon animal, which was the Elephant, calmed the disorder. The Monkeys reprimanded to the Chimpanzees that this is not their fault if they were impotent and could not produce. Only Buffalo refused to participate in the meeting because there were too many small animals which he did not like to befriend. The goal of the Tortoise was to find a way to fight against the massacre of men towards the animals. Many of the animals did not have the physical force to fight against the barbary of the man that was necessary to find a way to protect themselves. The Tortoise had already an idea in his head. He advised his companions to eat the core of the tree whose sap contained poison. The animal who would eat this core would not die but his flesh would be infected by the poison. The person who eats the flesh of the animal would die, because his flesh would already be infected by the poison.

From there, as the men were very intelligent, at the time they would understand the tip, they would leave us in peace. Then the Elephant inquired of the Tortoise if there were any side effects by eating the core of this tree. The Tortoise answered that there were no side effects, but in the beginning, you would get a little diarrhoea, the time your body would be getting accustomed to the presence of poison. The Elephant replicated that he would not eat the core because he did not like the diarrhoea. But Monkeys and the wild boar backed up and were most interested, also the Tortoise himself. Thus, these animals started to eat the poisoned core, without the villagers knowing about it. But in the future scientists found that the Ebola virus came from the flesh of the Monkey. Could we then make a connection with the disease Ebola and the flesh of other animals? We do not know, but the future would tell us if Ebola was from the flesh poisoning of Monkeys or other animals.

The time that the Chief and his nobles were thinking about the disappearance of the Tortoise, Master Tortoise came in front of them himself. The Chief and his nobles were afraid of the presence of the Tortoise, who returned to the hill.

The Tortoise asked the Chief, "I am here if you want my flesh".

But one of the nobles advised the Chief that he had to be careful with this animal, he was very dangerous. It was true that Tortoise was a wise animal and he wanted to leave his name to the future generation because he already ate the poisoned core to make the Chief perish. The Chief was surprised by the courage of the Tortoise who returned to the hill. Then the Chief told the Tortoise that he was free and announced a decree never to kill the Tortoise and to never eat the flesh of the Tortoise.

Let us come back to Mr Richard, the botanist. The mosquitoes of the village backed up, quite satisfied this time with the presence of the white man because, according to them he was fresh blood, different from the natives and villagers. And also, they had a green light to bite the foreign white man until he leaves the village. Having heard the news of the European, Felix, the mosquito who lived on the other side of the village came to visit his cousin, Abel. Last year, Abel was really weak and he could not manage to fly properly or bite people so he could nourish himself because of the sickness. But today, Felix found another Abel, well bearing, bronzing himself in the morning sun.

Felix shouted, "But Abel what health! Where has the miracle come from that you should be well bearing, because last year you were a dying mosquito?"

Able answered him with arrogance, "My food is different than yours and has many vitamins."

It was alluded to the blood of Richard that they sucked all night. But the cousin wanted to know exactly how his food had more vitamins. Then Able explained to his cousin that his customer, the European, did not eat mash cassava each day like the villagers but rather ate chocolate and milk. Then Felix told Abel he would not return home as long as he did not taste the delicious food from the white man.

"Look how I am not shinning; it looks like you contaminated me with your last year's disease."

Abel explained to his cousin that he could not bring him along because of the contract that they had signed with the village Chief. Felix rubbed his eyes with his two front legs to reject but decided not to give up and to contact the Chief in the night and ask if he could take part in the beverage. For making his cousin sicker, Abel took a glass of palm wine and started to drink with a straw, thinking it was impossible in this kind of environment. That was the straw that they stole from Richard, because the entire village knew that the white man drank juice with a straw and Abel wanted to impress his cousin Felix. Felix did not believe it, how Abel was now drinking differently.

Able answered him that wealth makes the difference. Abel advised his cousin that it would be very difficult for the Chief to give him the authorisation because this field was reserved to the mosquitoes of value and those who knew the techniques of fighting. Abel asked his cousin to give him a little bit of time to relax because his shift is during the night. But his cousin wanted to know more about the method of fighting. Abel gave him his reflection. Think a it a little bit like Donald Trump (the President of the USA), coming to visit Africa.

There were mosquitoes of value which still sucked the blood of the comrade President because his blood was not the same as all. It was necessary to have the method of fighting so you could suck the blood of the president. One of the ways was to cherish him before the bite, make him think that his wife is touching him.

Another technique was to never draw his attention to the presence of mosquitoes in his room because he was the best man to protect the world. People like Mr President were easy to bite because they were accustomed to sleep in acclimatised rooms, being unaware of the presence of an insect of value, especially mosquitoes. To hear the account of his cousin Felix who was sick because he did not know about everything his cousin was talking. He looked like a man without qualifications who came to seek a job. The Chief would not consider him because he did not have the necessary qualities to do the job.

On this side, Richard had received insecticides from his friend who worked in the embassy. However, Richard was unaware that the mosquitoes in this environment knew perfectly about insecticides and they had no fear. They also had a product to make the atmosphere pleasant. They waited at least an hour and with their fresh air, the atmosphere of the room became normal again and they started to bite again. This time they would bite him carefully to make him believe that the insecticides had worked. But in the morning, the victim realised that the state of his skin was deplorable. It was what happened to Richard; finally, he decided to leave the village. On his way he met a white priest. Richard also told him about his mishaps. He acknowledged that he could not live in this environment where mosquitoes were biting him all the night.

"The mosquitoes are ordered by somebody," the priest told him, "they have bitten you because the commander is not happy with you."

Richard asked, "Who can be the commander?"

The priest told him that he did not know but this kind of thing could not be unperceived by the Chief of the village, who could be himself the commander. Richard was surprised to hear that this man, the Chief, who was the father of Seraph could play a dirty trick. The priest advised him not to trust the appearance of anybody. They could be his enemy but they hid their animosity with their kindness.

"The villagers, when you greet them, very early in the morning, by saying 'Hello, Good Morning', they will answer you, 'Hello, Good Morning, too', followed by a poetic sentence that the heart of a man hides many things that you can't see. This means do not judge a man by his appearance because the heart can hide horrible things."

Richard explained to the priest that he couldn't even kill those mosquitoes with the insecticides. The priest burst out laughing, telling him that the mosquitoes could see everything he was doing and they had a system to protect themselves from the insecticides. It was true that there were things that the European couldn't understand. Initially, it was necessary to know the culture of the villagers and the natives to discover certain truths. There was a long conversation between the priest and Richard. The priest had many experiences and knew the mentality of the villagers. He had shared a long period of his life with these people. He advised Richard that the villagers communicated with some animals and insects.

Usually the villagers did not kill their enemy but threw a bad fate on him or make his life very difficult. Thus, it was necessary to avoid stealing goods of others and also avoid bathing in the river without the permission of the Chief because the Crocodiles and mosquitoes knew everybody who lived in the village. Before bathing in the village, he had to ask the permission of the Chief, and before serving fruit in a field, one had to ask the permission of the owner. He was sure the mosquitos that bit him was sent by someone who did not want Richard's presence there. So, Richard decided to leave the village very quickly. But first he went to greet the Chief and his friends. The children of the village were not happy to see Richard leaving.

The Chief, on his side, was looking to contact the Tortoise because the disappearance of this animal was making him sick in his heart. He didn't understand how the Tortoise could escape from the locked room. For him, the animal must have had magical power. The Chief convened all the nobles and asked them to bring back the Tortoise because he wanted to speak with him about a very serious problem. The Chief was like any leader, thirsty for power, wanting to discover the secret of the Tortoise and his magical power. The Tortoise was not afraid of anything, having already eaten the core, and with the decree of the Chief; it was a guaranteed surprise. He accepted with pleasure and he also wondered why the Chief wanted to see him. As a wise animal, he decided to follow the notables of the Chief. He arrived at the Chief's place and asked the notables if he could talk in private to the Chief. The Chief made his proposal to the Tortoise to deliver his magic power of how he could escape the locked jail. And the Tortoise, as wise as he was, directly understood the subject. The Tortoise answered the Chief and told him that this kind of thing was not spoken about like secret menu. He wanted to help but he had to contact the wizard of the village during the night and explain the problem. The wizard confirmed to the Tortoise that it was a small problem and he would make incantations on the Hippo, which the Chief would carry to make him believe that he became an invisible person. From that moment, many people started to wear amulets for the animals like the Leopard, Lion and the ivory of the Elephant or Rhino, believing to have power of magic. Most of them would see the wizard before they wear them.

Richard came to say goodbye to the Chief and explained that it was time to return to Europe but he regretted certain situations that he couldn't explain. The Chief answered him by a proverb, "when the bottle filled with oil is reverted, one cannot collect oil anymore and fill the bottle."

That meant to forget what happened in the past and look to the future. Richard did not understand the sense of this proverb and contradicted the Chief by bringing his bars of chocolate and when a chocolate fell, he collected it. He could not understand why the Chief spoke to him about the bottle of oil!

One notable shouted, "This white man is villainous, how can he contradict the Chief."

Richard carried on that he would return one day to continue the collection of the Butterflies. And at the same time, Seraph explained to his father that he was not a botanist, but he would return with Richard to continue his studies of medicine. The Chief and the notables were very frustrated that their native child was not a researcher of insects.

Seraph confirmed that he only came to show Richard the Butterflies of the village.

The Chief declared to one notable, "But we weren't supposed to send the mosquitoes," and the notable answered, "The oil is out of the bottle and therefore cannot be reversed."

END